To

Ben Tavernier

Contents

Kauō ulupau ka holo-kahiki.

A sailor drags his anchor in many harbors.

Hawaiian proverb

Tinfoil Angels

DECEMBER 7, 1941 was an unseasonably warm Sunday afternoon in Iowa. I was playing outdoors when a neighbor called from her backdoor and told me to tell my parents to turn on the radio because the "Japs" were invading America. I didn't know what "Japs" were and wasn't sure what "invading" was, but I knew from her voice that they weren't good.

I ran excitedly into the kitchen and told my mother the Japs were coming. She hurried to the living room where my father was reading a newspaper and told him the news. They turned on the radio and found a station reporting the Japanese attack on Pearl Harbor. I didn't understand most of what was said but I could tell it was serious.

Everyone in my hometown talked about the Pearl Harbor attack during the next few weeks. When I learned we weren't going to be invaded, my eight-year-old mind lost interest until I returned home from school one afternoon and found my mother crying. Her youngest brother had joined the army and she was afraid he would be killed in the war. Her oldest brother was killed in the Great War and she always said she hated wars. About two months after my uncle left, I learned that my father had applied for a civilian wartime job. He was eventually assigned to an army base in upstate New York called Pine Camp.

I loved the army base from the first day we arrived. Soldiers were everywhere. We lived in civilian housing on the base. I made friends easily and soon knew most of the kids my age. All colors, shapes and sizes, they came from everywhere in the U.S. One of them was at Pearl Harbor when the Japanese attacked and told scary stories about exploding bombs and dead people.

At school we kids were instructed in what we could do for the war effort. My neighborhood gang decided to specialize. Joey collected milkweed pods, Ken collected string, Irwin collected cellophane and I collected tinfoil. We weren't sure why we were collecting all this stuff, but our teacher told us it was important. The others eventually grew tired of collecting, but I became compulsive about picking up every discarded cigarette pack or gum wrapper I saw. I'd carefully peel off the thin foil and add it to my little ball that slowly grew with each addition.

The army base became a magical playground for us kids where we discovered hidden treasures in the dumps and trash bins that also yielded tinfoil for my growing ball. During the summer, we wandered the roads collecting pop and beer bottles, which we redeemed for two cents apiece—and, of course, I always found some tinfoil. Most of the boys smoked at our secret cave in the forest behind our houses, but I didn't care much for smoking and usually gave my cigarettes away but I always kept the empty packs for the tinfoil.

I saw my first movies at Pine Camp. The theater was nearby and admission was only a nickel. We boys joined the GIs in the long lines waiting to get in. Sometimes they picked us up and passed us from soldier to soldier to the front of the line. I always got a candy bar or two along the way. And, of course, I was partial to the ones with tinfoil wrappers.

We had our favorite soldiers at different places on the base and visited them routinely. At the gym we befriended a redheaded boxer. He sparred and wrestled with us on the big mat in the center of the gym. We ran through the obstacle course where GIs sometimes helped us over the more intimidating obstacles. When we visited the service club, the chubby Italian manager from Brooklyn gave us ice cream cones. Several soldiers learned I was collecting tinfoil and saved their cigarette and gum wrappers for me.

Visiting the hospital was another of our favorite activities. The hospital was a long, one-story building that stretched along the route we boys routinely wandered. During the first winter, we discovered that if we entered the hospital's back entrance we could walk its halls to the front, thereby avoiding a long walk in the cold. Some of the patients were from battlefronts, others were injured on base. Sometimes it took us a couple hours to get through the hospital as we stopped and talked to the patients. Some of them knew I collected tinfoil so I always left with additions to my expanding ball.

Each morning a bus transported us to school in a nearby little town and returned us in the afternoon. Friday was Bond Day when we took our dimes to school and bought stamps that we pasted into our savings books. At some future date, we would have enough stamps to buy a war bond. I wasn't sure how, but I knew that somehow I was helping America win the war.

But tinfoil was my passion. Each time my tinfoil reached the size of a baseball I took it to school and gave it to my teacher. She would show it to the class and call me to the front of the room. I was always embarrassed, but it made me feel good to know that my tinfoil was saving someone's life. I hadn't the foggiest idea how it was saving lives, but I firmly believed it was. Maybe it was used to make airplanes, maybe guns and bullets, maybe bombs or ships or tanks or jeeps.

Then I would go home and start another ball.

Although I was told they were only practice, the air raid drills frightened me. We were ushered into the school basement until the all-clear signal sounded. The teacher said we were too far away from the battlegrounds to be concerned about real air raids, but I wasn't sure.

And then as suddenly as it began, the war ended. I was glad the war was over, but I missed collecting tinfoil. For a long time, I found it difficult to resist the shiny tinfoil of a discarded gum wrapper or cigarette package.

Fast forward sixty years.

My anthropological colleague Paul Jardin invited me several times to visit him at his family's farm in Belgium.

He and his wife lived in the Philippines when I first met them, but periodically they spent summers in Belgium with Paul's large extended family in a small village nestled on the flank of a hill near Liège. This time the logistics worked. I flew into Brussels, rented a car and drove through the rolling countryside of eastern Belgium to Paul's village located on the fringes of the historic Battle of the Bulge, the World War II battle when Germany made a final major effort to stem the invading allied forces.

The farm was even more charming than Paul promised. The imposing Eighteenth Century farmhouse presided over a collection of outbuildings that included a big stone barn housing the family dairy. Resting at the edge of the village, the farm joined rolling green pastures dotted with other farmsteads and occasional clusters of forest. The Battle of the Bulge cast its long shadow over much of the countryside with museums, cemeteries and historical markers commemorating the brutal battle. Paul and I lived through the war as children on our separate continents and unsurprisingly, our conversation occasionally returned to those years.

Paul was a teenager during the war and his experiences would fill a trilogy of action movies. He was at boarding school when the Germans invaded Belgium and with other youths was sent home. However, when he and a classmate started home on their bicycles, they discovered the invading Germans blocking their way. They headed the opposite direction, slept in barns and fields and begged food from farmers and villagers along the way. They ended up at Dunkirk where they witnessed the evacuation of British troops by the ragtag flotilla that

England sent across the channel to rescue its desperate men. The boys attempted to board one of the boats but were rejected because the precious space was reserved for British soldiers only. Following a rainy night in an open field, they again found themselves facing the advancing German army and remained hidden as it passed. The next morning they hitched a ride on a train and were almost killed when it was bombed by the Germans. They fled the carnage left by strafing airplanes and eventually escaped through gaps in the enemy lines, finally reaching their home village.

Following a tearful but happy reunion with his family, Paul joined the Belgian underground, sabotaging German installations and under the cover of night escorting fleeing Jews to safe havens. He helped his fellow villagers bury the local church bell in the nearby forest before the Germans confiscated it for scrap metal. After the allied invasion of Normandy, American troops eventually reached Paul's village and several months later the fierce Battle of the Bulge was raging a few miles away. The village and family farm became a sanctuary for the allied soldiers, mostly Americans, who escaped the nearby battlefields for a few hours of respite. Paul's family befriended the GIs who slept in their barn and in gratitude, the GIs shared their K-rations, cigarettes and chocolate bars.

On the eve of my departure, Paul's sister Marie hosted a farewell dinner in my honor at her charming cottage. Following the delicious meal and good wine, our conversation once again returned to the war years and their influence on our childhoods. I recalled my years at the army base, my compulsive tinfoil-collecting and my fear of attack during the air raid drills.

Paul's family remembered the real thing—the day the German soldiers arrived to occupy their village, the unrelenting sounds of battle a few miles away, planes strafing the countryside and occasionally dropping bombs. And finally the arrival of the American and British troops at the nearby warfront that history would remember as The Battle of the Bulge.

Following a pause in the conversation, Marie recalled the Christmas of 1944. A lean holiday was approaching and the family was resigned that it would be a day not much different from the battle-scarred days of the past several weeks. The day before Christmas, twelve-year-old Marie and her younger brother were playing in a field near the barn. The sounds of battle blasted nearby, but by now they were familiar sounds and did not disrupt the children's play. German and Allied planes occasionally streaked through the skies, but they, too, had become commonplace and hardly warranted comment. As the children romped through the fresh snow in the first sunshine after many gray days, thin strips of silver began drifting earthward from the sky, a shower of sparkling silver from the heavens. They excitedly plucked the strips from the air and gathered them from the snow.

The children discussed the possible origin of the silver strips and concluded they were gifts from the angels in heaven. They took the strips home where they met their father talking with two GIs in the barnyard. They showed the silver strips to their father who was as puzzled as they concerning their origins. One of the GIs, however, explained that the tinfoil strips were routinely dropped by allied planes to disrupt the radio waves of the Germans. Uninterested in this secular explanation, the children took their heavenly-sent treasures into the house. They found cardboard, cut it into two angel shapes and carefully swathed them with the tinfoil strips. On Christmas morning, they presented the tinfoil angels to their family, the only gifts in the household during that bleak, war-weary Christmas. Their mother placed the angels in the center of the dining table and led family prayers asking for an end to the war and happier future Christmases.

Marie concluded her story and we silently entertained our individual memories of the war years. Marie quietly left the room. Minutes later she returned with a small box containing mementos from the war, including several letters from grateful GIs after they returned home. She passed the letters to me and as I read them, she retrieved a small parcel wrapped in yellowed tissue paper at the bottom of the box. She gently unwrapped it to reveal two crudely shaped angels about six inches tall covered in strips of tinfoil. She handed them to me.

As I quietly and cautiously examined the fragile silver angels, I wondered if the tinfoil that enswathed them was collected by that boy in upstate New York who once was me.

Loss at Sea

WHEN I STEPPED from the airplane and felt the warm moist tropical midnight air on my face, I knew Hawaii was the right decision. And when I descended the airstairs and smelled the scent of ginger and plumeria from the Hawaiian lei-sellers on the tarmac, I was even more convinced. Propeller flights still flew to Hawaii in those early days of the 1960s and they were a lot cheaper than jets. My student budget had encapsulated me for hours in one of the ancient planes and any place would have seemed great after the claustrophobia of the interminable flight. But Hawaii was even more than I hoped for.

Graduate study in anthropology brought me to the islands. Polynesia was my chief interest back then and my main reason for choosing the University of Hawaii was Zara Zakata, one of the outstanding scholars on Polynesia. But Zara Zakata and anthropology were far from my mind when I spotted Jan. She broke from the crowd and placed a lei around my neck as we embraced in a warm hug. A local Filipina friend from my undergraduate days, Jan initially spurred my interest in Hawaii and things anthropological. We said the sorts of things good friends say when they haven't seen one another for a long time and then found the baggage area, located the suitcase containing all my worldly possessions and were soon speeding through a light industrial district toward Honolulu. We ended up in a Chinese restaurant with the unlikely name "McCully Chop Sui" where I was introduced to island-style Cantonese cuisine.

I stayed with Jan four days. The first day she played tour-guide on a grand tour of Oahu. As we circled the pre-freeway island, she pointed out scenic and historic sites. The second day we wandered pre-highrise Honolulu and spent the late afternoon on an empty beach at the Diamond Head-end of Waikiki. The third day I began apartment hunting, never my favorite thing to do, but in those days it was exacerbated by blatant discrimination. Landlords advertised for Japanese only, Filipinos only, Hawaiians only or haoles only. I persevered and eventually found a tiny, grubby studio apartment. The rent suited my limited student means and it was within easy walking distance to the university. Jan helped me move in and then left for the opening school term on the Big Island where she taught. That evening I unpacked my suitcase and lay back on a saggy bed to watch geckos devour cockroaches on the grimy walls. I was in Hawaii and I was so damn happy to be there.

Fall semester began the following Monday. My first class was "Polynesia" with Zara Zakata. I arrived early to get a seat at the back and as the room filled to capacity I was glad I was early. Students entered, searched for familiar faces and finding none sat down quietly. At one minute before nine, we heard a door shut down the hall followed by light, but determined footsteps. At exactly nine o'clock, Zara Zakata entered the classroom.

Not an expression changed, but everyone was somewhat taken aback. Her name prepared us for an exotic, voluptuous siren, perhaps Middle Eastern, with piles of dark hair and loads of jewelry. The real Zara Zakata was a shy, diminutive Caucasian woman, very blond and blue-eyed, in her mid-fifties. She wore low-heeled white shoes and a pale blue cotton dress of floral print. She looked at the floor as she entered the room, walked to the lectern, opened a folder and announced that she would read the class roster. She read our names, occasionally asking if her pronunciation was correct. She then counted out syllabi and handed them to a student sitting in the seat nearest her. So far he was the only student she looked at, and it was a quick glance. She announced that everything we needed to know about the class was in the syllabus, that she strictly enforced her office hours and saw students only at that time. Then she began lecturing in a soft monotone about the geography of Polynesia without once glancing up from her notes. At exactly ten minutes of ten, she stopped lecturing almost in mid-sentence, closed her folder and left the room. More than a few students grumbled about her teaching style as we vacated the classroom.

That first class set the pace for the semester. Her lectures were always delivered in a quiet monotone that lulled most of the class to sleep. But those of us who stayed awake discovered that the lectures were crammed with information. Her exams were killers. She believed we needed to know the facts of Polynesia before we could begin theorizing about them. And we certainly got the facts. Polynesia was my passion in those years and I couldn't get enough of it.

Most students, however, didn't share my enthusiasm. They found her lectures boring and resented the details of her exams. I aced the course and loved every minute of it.

As the semester progressed, I discovered that Zara Zakata's exotic name was anglicized Hungarian. Her short, softly waved hair was probably naturally blond, but she assisted it with periodic treatments that were as predictable as most of her life. She wore four dresses of identical style to class, floral prints in pastel colors—pink, blue, green and yellow, always in that sequence. She met her classes on Monday, Wednesday and Friday, and only the greatest emergencies brought her to campus on Tuesday or Thursday when she exercised at the YWCA near her sparsely furnished apartment in Waikiki.

Zara Zakata was not a fieldworker. During the late 1940s she spent three unpleasant months on a remote island in the Tuamotus, but most of her research was in the university library. She published extensively on every aspect of Polynesia and anyone researching the area had to first deal with what she had written. She never taught summer session and rarely remained in Hawaii during those months. She loved travel and always timed her trips with a conference so she could present one of the many papers she was always writing—and also so she could write off the trip as a professional expense for tax purposes. Her pecuniary practices were legendary. She didn't own a car and always walked to campus because she resented the bus fare, but grudgingly paid it when she returned home in the late afternoon. She brought her lunch each day rather than pay what she considered exorbitant prices in the cafeteria.

During office hours, her door was open about a foot—sometimes less if she was in a foul mood. As soon as the hour ended, the door was closed and no student dared disturb her. Most were terrified of her. They rarely asked questions during class since it was obvious she did not want her lectures interrupted. However, if someone asked a good question, she responded in great depth, providing sources to pursue in the library. But she had no patience with foolish questions. Once a haole surfer who somehow stumbled into her class asked why some Hawaiians resented being part of the United States since it was such a great democratic country. She had just finished a lecture on the illegal U.S. overthrow of the Hawaiian monarchy in the late 19th century. She stared at him levelly for a moment, one of the longest eye contacts she made, and said quietly, "Mr. Nelson, you suffer from serious delusions of adequacy in this class," then returned to her lecture.

Zara Zakata was the most conscientious professor I ever had, never late for class and never absent. Essay exams and research papers were read at least twice and marked extensively. I came to her class with a good writing background and prided myself on being rather capable with the pen. The first written assignment she returned knocked me down to size: it dripped in red comments and corrections as if she'd severed a major artery and saturated the pages.

The summer of my first year in Hawaii, Zara Zakata attended a conference in Tahiti on ethnographic research in the Pacific. She planned a two-week trip but ended up staying until late summer. I knew this because I had persuaded her to sit on my dissertation committee and she reluctantly agreed to discuss my research proposal when she returned from Tahiti. She reminded me that she was paid to teach two semesters and seeing students during summer session was not part of her contract. I humbly thanked her for condescending to see me gratis. In late July, I received a short note telling me she had changed her plans and would not be in Honolulu until the week before fall semester. She hoped it would not inconvenience me. It didn't.

The week following her return to campus I went to her office. The door was wide open. She was seated at her desk and momentarily I thought I was in the wrong office. She wore a tailored navy blue suit with a white blouse ruffled at the neck. Her hair was lighter and cut in an attractive pageboy style. High heels showed off attractive calves I'd never noticed before. She smiled warmly and invited me in.

"And how was your summer?" she asked, clearing papers from a chair so I could sit. Piles of papers and books covered her desk. It was the first time I'd seen anything out of order in her office. "I'm sorry I was unable to make our appointment in July."

"No problem," I said. "I fell behind schedule anyway. How was Tahiti?"

"Tahiti was marvelous," she said. "I shall certainly be going back."

"And was the conference good?"

"The conference?" She looked puzzled. "Oh yes, the conference. Of course!" She laughed. "So long ago it slipped my mind. It was quite good. My paper was well received. I had such a good time enjoying Tahiti that I almost forgot the conference. Now what can I do for you?"

"I'd like to leave a copy of my dissertation proposal and make an appointment to discuss it."

"Of course. Let me check my calendar." She did so and we made an appointment for the following week.

I wasn't the only one who noticed the change in Zara Zakata. The department was abuzz. She was actually late for class a couple of times and made eye contact while lecturing—and even told jokes. She entertained questions and strayed from the lecture topic on several occasions, and one day she actually sat on the desk while lecturing. She wore several non-pastel outfits to class. As she walked down the hall, she looked directly at students, smilingly wishing them good morning or good afternoon. Once she came in on Tuesday and on another occasion she was seen on campus during the weekend.

The following week I arrived at Zara Zakata's office for our appointment. She was sitting on her desk, humming while paging through a magazine. I'd never seen her read a magazine before, and I'd certainly never heard her hum. She looked up smilingly and then with slight alarm.

"Oh dear. You're here for our appointment, aren't you? I'm so embarrassed. I forgot the appointment and haven't read your proposal yet. I've been rather busy."

"No problem," I said. It really was no problem but I was somewhat taken aback. I couldn't believe that Zara Zakata forgot an appointment and didn't have a student paper ready on time.

"Could you make it Friday at this time?"

"Sure. That'll be fine."

She held up the magazine and said, "I'm considering buying an automobile and I've been reading *Consumer Reports* about the different models. It's very confusing when you know nothing about automobiles. Do you know much about them?"

I admitted ignorance about cars and left after a few more words.

On Friday, I arrived at Zara Zakata's office at the appointed time. This time she was ready. She had read my proposal carefully and we spent an hour discussing it. She was back to her old self (except for the red dress she wore) and had disagreed with some of my theoretical positions. She also noted that the date of one of my bibliographic entries was off a year. It was a good session and I appreciated anew her critical thoroughness. I thanked her and as I stood to leave, a tall good-looking man, probably in his mid- fifties, appeared at the door. He had a short white beard and warm brown eyes.

"I'm afraid I'm early," he said on seeing me.

"We're just finishing," said Professor Zakata. "This is the student I was telling you about who is planning fieldwork in the Sulu Islands." She introduced him as her friend Chet Robersin.

"I spent time in Sulu in the early fifties," he said. "What island do you plan to visit?"

"The Tawi-Tawi area. Were you there?"

"Never made it down there. Only as far as Jolo."

"Someplace in the Pacific where you haven't been?" laughed Professor Zakata. "I find that hard to believe."

"I've missed a couple of islands," he said, smiling at her. "I was only in Sulu a few days. You'll enjoy your stay there. Beautiful islands and interesting people."

"I'm looking forward to it," I said. We exchanged farewells and I left.

Chet Robersin became a familiar figure around the department that semester. He usually appeared in mid-afternoon and waited for Professor Zakata to finish her last class. Sometimes he waited in the student lounge where he reminisced with students about his Pacific travels. Originally from Maine, he had navigated ships in the Pacific since the end of World War II when he spent time in the Solomon Islands with the navy. He loved the Pacific and had no desire to live elsewhere. Hawaii was too far north and too American for his taste. He had come up to spend a few weeks with Zara Zakata while his ship underwent extensive refurbishing in Tahiti. No wife was ever mentioned, but he intimated to some of the male students that he'd had his share of women in the Pacific and probably a few of his children were scattered among the islands. He was a likeable character but like a lot of straight men, he spent too much time confirming his *machismo* for my taste.

No one could figure out his relationship with Zara Zakata, but it was assumed a romantic one. They appeared together at the annual luau hosted each September by the department and sat on a blanket slightly away from the rest of the group laughing and talking.

A student rumor claimed they met in Papeete when she attended the conference there the previous summer. Another said they were old school friends reunited in Papeete where their earlier friendship blossomed into romance. However it transpired, we were happy about it. Zara Zakata was a different woman. Her lectures were more interesting and she was much more approachable. As far as we were concerned, if this was romance, *Viva la romance.*

Chet Robersin stayed in Honolulu until the first of the year. I occasionally saw him in the library's Pacific Collection poring over the old journals of European explorers. He once told me he was reading early accounts of some of the islands he'd visited. Several times I engaged him in conversation about his travels in the Pacific, but he didn't have a lot to say. For someone who had visited so many exotic places, he had absorbed very little and understood them only superficially. He seemed a strange mate for Zara Zakata who knew perhaps more about the Pacific than anyone else in the world. I wondered what her attraction to him was. But I long ago learned that Cupid works in strange ways and Eros works in even weirder ones.

He apparently left during semester break. At any rate, he was gone when the second semester began. When a bold student asked Zara Zakata where he was, she replied that he had returned to Tahiti to command his ship. She purchased several new outfits over the holidays and sometimes went eight classes before repeating the same dress. She continued smiling and greeting people in the hallways. And her sense of humor, which no one suspected before, spiced her lectures. Her office door was wide open during office hours and she frequently invited passing students to visit.

All went well until early April. Then the dark clouds began gathering.

The first hint of something wrong was when Zara Zakata stopped smiling and began staring at the floor again as she walked between her office and classroom. Her lectures once again became dull monotones and her sense of humor evaporated. Her new clothes disappeared and the predictable rotation of the four pastels returned. The stylish shoes were replaced with her sensible low-heeled white ones and her office door was open only a few inches during office hours. The little cloud of unhappiness returned above her. A few days later, the reason appeared in the *Honolulu Advertiser*.

I was reading the newspaper before going to campus one morning and discovered a brief story in the inside pages under "Pacific News." The *Rising Star*, an inter-island trading vessel containing twenty passengers and four crewmembers disappeared between Tahiti and the Marquesas. It was two weeks overdue in Papeete and search ships and planes were unable to locate it. Chet Robersin was captain of the missing ship.

I was not the only one who read the story. The entire department was talking about it when I arrived on campus that afternoon. Zara Zakata was on campus also. She met with her classes but her door remained closed during office hours. Late that afternoon, I met her in the hallway as she was leaving her office. She did not look up when I approached her, but I spoke anyway.

"I am very sorry about the news of Captain Robersin," I said.

She looked at me, said nothing and then looked at the floor again.

"Surely the ship will be found soon," I added.

"Surely," she said without looking up. She turned and walked away.

The *Rising Star* became a hot item in the local as well as the international presses. The search continued but no trace of the ship was found. An enterprising reporter discovered it was registered in the name of Zara Zakata and managed to interview her. She told him she had invested in the ship with Chet Robersin as a business venture they hoped to expand throughout the central Pacific. She had no explanation for the disappearance and only knew that Robersin had returned to Tahiti to take the ship on its first voyage after its renovation.

As the weeks passed and the *Rising Star* was not found, speculation about what happened to it flourished.

Explanations ranged from pirates to outer space visitors. Some suggested a freak storm sank it but records revealed no evidence of bad weather in the area. As each new story appeared, Professor Zakata was asked to comment on it. She made a brief statement to discount suggestions that Captain Robersin was holding the passengers hostage for ransoms. A couple days later, she said she did not think a competitor had pirated the ship. About a week later, a story appeared claiming the ship was uninsured which deflated a theory that it was sunk to collect insurance money. Zara Zakata then stopped talking. Reporters tried to interview her but she refused to see them.

After a month of lurid speculation about the *Rising Star*'s whereabouts, the lifeboat from the ship was discovered midway between Tahiti and the Marquesas. No one was on board. The search was intensified. Planes and ships combed the open seas and every island of the area searching for the missing ship and its passengers. Nothing was found.

Speculations became even more sensational and the media had a field day with the story. Reporters hounded Zara Zakata, but she still refused to comment. They waited outside her apartment and followed her to campus. They talked to students to see if she had said something about the incident in her classes. Secretaries, professors and janitors were interviewed. But Zara Zakata said nothing to anyone.

Everyone in the department, of course, was as curious about the incident as the rest of the world. A student, more ballsy than bright, asked Professor Zakata during class if she had any idea what happened to the missing passengers. She glared at him, gathered her notes and left the classroom. No one considered broaching the subject with her after that. She became even more isolated from the department. A few of us tried to express our sympathy, but she rebuffed our efforts and let us know she was uninterested in any sympathy we had to offer.

The *Rising Star* eventually disappeared from the front pages. Occasionally new speculations appeared about the lost passengers but they were relegated to inside pages. Both the French and U.S. governments made official investigations but neither offered any enlightenment about the missing ship. Inquiries were eventually closed with officials admitting they had no explanation for the incident.

As the years rolled by, new students and faculty came and went in the department. One of the first things they learned was to never mention anything about the *Rising Star* in Zara Zakata's presence. She eventually shed some of the gloom she carried during the early months of the ship's disappearance, but she never again became the person she was when Chet Robersin was part of her life. She fell back into the familiar patterns of my early graduate school days.

I finished my PhD and returned to the Mainland for an academic position in California. But as with everyone who has ever lived in Hawaii, I never totally left the islands. I returned frequently and each time I did, I spent time with Zara. She had been an important mentor during my student days and when I entered professional anthropology, I acquired new respect for her accomplishments as our friendship evolved. I never asked about the *Rising Star* or mentioned Chet Robersin, assuming they were painful subjects for her.

The *Rising Star* disappeared from the newspapers, but it was too good a story to be forgotten. Periodically, some writer heard about it and rehashed it one more time. Occasionally someone tried to interview Zara, but she refused to speak to them. Two very bad adventure-mystery type books were written about it, and a grade B movie was loosely based on the story that is remembered today only because a currently popular movie star made her screen debut as a sexy Zara Zakata. The story became part of South Pacific lore and almost everyone living there knows a version of it. One widespread legend claims that on the anniversary of its disappearance, the *Rising Star* appears in a bank of fog and for a few frightening moments, the moan of its horn and the wailing cries of its lost passengers are heard. Then it disappears as quickly as it appeared. Zara became an increasingly romantic figure in the story and her perennial sadness was attributed to her lost lover on the lost ship.

After Zara retired from teaching, she retained an office at the university and continued research and writing. She occasionally sat on dissertation committees, but for the most part she removed herself from active participation in the department.

A week before Zara died, I lunched with her in Honolulu. I met her in the lobby of her apartment building and we drove to her favorite restaurant in Moiliili. We sat near a pool where she could watch the colorful *koi.* She had once raised tropical fish and had a long-standing interest in all fish. She had, of course, written about Polynesian attitudes toward fish. I asked about her current research and she told me she recently completed a paper that had given her a great deal of trouble. She was so exasperated by it that she vowed not to start another for at least a month. I couldn't imagine her not working on a paper but said nothing. Our conversation moved to the past and people from my early days at the university. She maintained an active interest in her favorite students and usually knew their whereabouts.

"That was a long time ago," she mused during a pause in our conversation. "The years have gone by so swiftly. It's sometimes difficult to keep them in order." She paused. "I usually measure my life by 'B.R.S.' or 'A.R.S.'—'before the *Rising Star*' and 'after the *Rising Star*'."

I almost choked on my wine. It was the first time I'd heard her mention the *Rising Star.* I couldn't let such an opportunity pass.

"Do you have any thoughts about what happened to the *Rising Star*?"

"Who knows? I long ago gave up thinking about it. *What* happened to it was not my major concern. My concern was that it *happened.*"

"Captain Robersin's disappearance must have been a terrible blow for you."

"It was certainly terrible that he and all those others died." She hesitated. "But it was the loss of the ship—not Robersin—that was a terrible blow for me. That ship was supposed to make us a fortune. Robersin talked me into sinking every dollar I had into that damn ship. He spent the insurance money I gave him and never insured it. I was an idiot to invest in one of his harebrained schemes. I should've known he'd end up sinking it. He always was a fool. I planned to retire early from teaching and spend all my time in research and writing. I hated teaching."

She picked up the dessert menu and studied it for several moments. "I think I'll have the coconut cake."

I ordered the lemon meringue pie.

Patterns of Culture

IT WAS A chilly, foggy Monday evening in San Francisco. After a long, tiring day on campus, I stopped by the YMCA to soak up some steam before going home to vegetate in front of the TV until bedtime. I pulled off my clothes and stuffed them into a locker. Sitting on a stool a couple of lockers away, a young man dressed in workout clothes was lacing up his gym shoes while giving my crotch a serious appraisal.

He smiled at me. I smiled back. Another time I might've been more encouraging, but I was too tired for sex. In those days, that was *really* tired. He was a good-looking guy with golden brown skin, black hair and almond eyes. He could've come from any of the millions of square miles of Asia or Latin America.

I wrapped my towel around my waist and headed for the steam room. When I opened the door, a cloud of hot, moist air hit me. I stepped inside, closed the door and adjusted to the steamy room. I found a space on the bench and my tense body responded to the seductive steam as I closed my eyes and drained my head of matters academic.

I sensed more than saw someone sit beside me. Slowly, a knee pressed mine. I moved, thinking I was taking too much space. Moments later I felt the knee again. It wasn't that crowded. I eased my leg away, opened my eyes and glanced toward the pressure. Beside me was the golden young man I'd seen in the locker room. He'd obviously changed his mind about working out. He flashed me a broad smile. I smiled back and pulled my knees closer together. Public cruising has never been my thing.

The steam was getting to me, so I left the room and entered the shower room. As I lathered up, my new admirer came in and took the shower beside me. He lathered his trim, attractive body into a semi-erection. The shower room was crowded and no one missed what was going on. His heavy cruise embarrassed me. I rinsed off and entered the drying room to towel down. He was on my heels. I finished drying and returned to the locker room. He was right behind me.

As he dried his hair beside me, he said, "Do you work out here often?"

"Every other day. But tonight I'm too tired for a work-out. It's been a long day."

"My name's Leland," he said, holding out his hand. He spoke with a slight accent I couldn't identify.

I told him my name and shook his hand. He squeezed it warmly and held on a bit longer than customary.

"Would you like to join me upstairs for a cup of coffee?"

"I'd like to," I said, "but I'm really bushed. I gotta get home before I collapse."

"Maybe another time," he suggested.

"Yeah. Maybe another time." I finished dressing and gave him a wave as I left the locker room. He punctuated his smile with a wink and waved back.

I forgot about him as I fought traffic to get home.

About a week later I was at the Y again. I was finishing my last weight machine when Leland entered the room. He saw me and headed my way.

"Good to see you," he said as he began warm-up stretches. "I was hoping I'd run into you. How about getting together after workout? I'll buy you a drink."

This time I wasn't tired. "Six o'clock in the lobby?" I suggested.

"I'll be there."

He disappeared into the weight room. I finished my final routine and ran a half-hour on the indoor jogging track. After showering, I went to the lobby where Leland was waiting.

"The bars are mobbed at this hour. How about coming to my place?" he suggested. "It'll be more conducive to talking."

I knew talking wasn't what he had in mind, but it wasn't what I had in mind either so I agreed to meet him at the address he gave me. He was sitting on the front steps of his apartment building when I pulled up.

We went inside and were in bed before a drink was poured. He had the looks, the body and the passion, but that special something that makes it really happen wasn't there for either of us. Still it was a good encounter and afterwards we stretched out on his king-size bed.

"Where're you from?" I asked. "I can't place your accent."

"Guess."

"I wouldn't know where to begin. The possibilities are too great."

He laughed. "I'm from Singapore. I'm Chinese with some Portuguese and Malay on my mother's side."

"How long you been in San Francisco?"

"Almost three years. Aren't you going to tell me how good my English is?"

I smiled. I wasn't going to say so, but his English was better than many Chinese immigrants I knew.

"Okay," I said. "Your English is great."

"Thanks. I've worked at it."

"What kind of work do you do?"

"International banking. I'm with one of the big banks downtown. How about you?"

"I'm an anthropologist."

"The next question is usually, 'Do you have a lover?'"

I laughed. "Not at the moment. How about you?"

"No," he said. "But not because I don't want one. I don't like being alone."

"Are you here for good, or are you going back to Singapore?"

"I'd like to be here for good." He paused. "But someday before too long I've got to go back. I'm the only son and there's a family business I'm expected to take over. After San Francisco, Singapore is like the Middle Ages."

I'd been in Singapore several times and knew its antediluvian attitudes toward gays. Nonetheless I asked, "Can you live there as a gay man?"

"No way. When I go back I stop being gay."

"Not easy to do," I said. "Does your family know you're gay?"

"If they do, they choose to ignore it. They're too busy trying to find a wife for me. They expect me to come back and marry and have sons."

"And what are your plans?"

"I don't have a lot of choice," he said.

"The world's full of choices."

He was quiet for a moment and then said, "You don't know my Chinese family."

Leland and I never had sex again, but we continued to see one another. He was a bright guy and had some interesting insights into American culture. He was also obviously lonely and didn't have a lot of friends. We occasionally met for dinner and periodically saw a film together. Sometimes we ran into one another at the Y and worked out together. One evening after not seeing him for several weeks, I called to ask if he wanted to see a film that recently opened. We had discussed it earlier and he'd expressed interest in it.

"How'd you like to see *Red Sunset*?" I said after initial greetings. "It's playing at the Castro."

"Good timing," he said. "I'm free for the weekend. Does Saturday night work for you?"

"Sounds good. How about dinner before the movie? It starts at eight."

We decided on a German restaurant not far from the theater and arranged to meet there.

* * *

When I arrived at the restaurant Leland was seated at a window table with a glass of white wine. I ordered a beer and we made small talk as we watched the always-watchable crowd that stalks that part of Market Street.

After we ordered, Leland announced with a broad smile, "I found the man I've been looking for."

"Congratulations," I said, somewhat surprised. He hadn't mentioned a boyfriend to me. "That doesn't happen for too many people. Who is he?"

"His name's Rod. I met him at the Y. Maybe you've seen him there."

He described him, but it was no one I remembered.

"So it looks like something serious?" I asked.

"Really serious," he said. "He's a nice guy and great sex."

The waiter brought our salads. After he left, Leland continued. "He's an attorney. Works in international law."

"Sounds compatible to your international finance."

"Yes, it is. We talk a lot of the same language. He spent time in Malaya when he was in the Peace Corps. You and he are about the only Americans I know who've heard of Kuala Lumpur. He has a feel for Asia that's hard to find among most Americans."

"How long you been together?"

"Almost two weeks. We've been together every night since we met. He's in Chicago for a funeral this weekend; otherwise I wouldn't be here with you—nothing personal."

I laughed. "I understand. I've been there."

The waiter took the empty salad plates and brought our entrées. Leland told me more about his boyfriend as we ate. He was obviously quite smitten. When dessert arrived, we realized we were running late. We gobbled our *streuselkuchen*, paid the bill and hurried to the theater.

About two weeks later, I returned to my darkened flat after a long day at the university. I found some light and turned on the blinking answering machine.

"Hi, this is Leland. Are you free Saturday for dinner? I want you to meet Rod. Seven o'clock. I'll cook something Malay."

I dialed his number and got his answering machine. Leland's voice told me, "You have reached the residence of Leland Wong and Rodney Langers. Please leave a message and we will return your call."

Things were moving fast.

I left a message saying I was free for dinner and would see them Saturday.

Leland met me at the door Saturday night. We hugged and I handed him a bottle of wine.

"If it doesn't work with dinner, save it for another time."

"It'll work great," he said. "Come in and meet Rod."

I followed him to the living room where a blond man, probably in his middle thirties, stood near the mantel. Leland introduced us and we shook hands. Rod said he'd seen me at the Y, but I didn't recognize him. He was a pleasant man—not great looking, not bad. Leland excused himself to the kitchen and Rod and I talked about the Y and discovered people we knew in common. I asked him about his stint in the Peace Corps. He was in Malaya about the same time I did my early fieldwork in the southern Philippines. We knew some of the same places and were reminiscing about Sulawesi when Leland announced dinner.

We entered the dining room and confronted a beautiful array of Malay dishes, and soon discovered their taste equaled their looks. I didn't know Leland was a cook and told him so.

"I love to cook," he said. "If I had my choice, I'd be a chef."

"Why not pursue it?" I asked. "You certainly have the talent."

"The family has other things in mind for me." He changed the subject. "Did you guys discover anyone you knew in common in Asia? You were there at the same time."

"No," laughed Rod. "Asia's a big place. But we visited some of the same places."

We talked more about Asia and the pleasant evening passed rapidly. I always enjoy talking about Asia, and both Leland and Rod knew a lot about that huge, diverse chunk of the world. They were obviously very much in love, all the big and little signs were there. Rod had moved in two weeks previously and the honeymoon was in full swing.

At midnight I looked at the clock. Surprised to find it so late, I quickly took my leave.

*　　*　　*

I didn't see a lot of Leland and Rod after that dinner. I occasionally ran into them at the Y and sometimes worked out with them. They moved beyond the honeymoon to a healthy, loving relationship. They were inseparable. During that first winter, they skied at Tahoe almost every other weekend and spent a week in Hawaii. They moved from Leland's apartment to a large flat in Pacific Heights which they furnished in a style as comfortable as their relationship. They attended the symphony and were regulars at the ballet. In the spring, they went to New York for a week of theater. They seemed the perfect couple and almost everyone who knew them secretly envied them.

One evening after a day of university-type things at home, I went to the Y for a vigorous workout. I worked the weight machines and then ran for an hour on the indoor track. I returned to the workout room and collapsed on the mat to collect my energy before going downstairs to shower. As I lay on my back, looking up at the almost-century of remodeling and repair on the ceiling, someone sat beside me. It was Rod.

"Good to see you," I said. "It's been a while. What you been up to?"

"Same old stuff. Busy at work."

"How's Leland?"

He shrugged. "He's Leland." He paused and stretched out beside me. "We had our first really big fight. I came here to get away."

"Sorry," I said. "I guess a few of them come with the turf in any relationship."

"I suppose," he said. "This one's been building for a while." He raised his right leg, grabbed his shin with both hands and pulled it toward him.

I waited for him to continue.

"It's the family thing," he said.

"His family?"

"Yes. They want him to return to Singapore and start taking charge of the business."

"And what does he want?"

"He says he doesn't have any choice. That he owes it to them."

"What about you?"

"He wants me to go back with him."

"He's told them about you?"

"Of course not," he said. "He's totally in the closet back there."

"How's he going to explain his American roommate to the family?"

"It's more complicated than that. They've lined up a bride for him."

"This *is* getting complicated."

"There's more. He wants me to transfer to Singapore and get an apartment where he'll come and see me when he can slip away from his family."

"Sounds like he wants to have his proverbial cake and eat it too."

"You got that right. He keeps telling me he loves me and will never love anyone else. But he owes it to his family to go back and have children."

"That's important in his culture."

"What about me? I have a few needs too."

"I'm not denying that," I said. "I'm just trying to tell you where Leland's coming from."

"I love the bastard," he said, tears brimming in his eyes. "I've never loved anyone so much in my life."

"I'm sorry. Love's always complicated, but even more so when it crosses cultures," I said anthropologically.

"He keeps telling me he loves me."

"I've always thought so," I said.

"He obviously loves his family more."

"I'm not sure it's love. More like an obligation, one he was weaned on."

He sat up and said, "Sorry to spill my problems all over you." He wiped his eyes.

"I wish I could be more helpful. Give me a call if you want to talk about it more."

"Thanks," he said as he stood. "I better get home. Leland will be worried."

About a week later, on a Saturday, I got a call from Leland.

"How about coffee this afternoon?"

"Sure," I said. "Just the two of us?"

"Yes. Rod's at a conference in L.A."

I suggested a recently opened coffeehouse in the Lower Haight, the current in-place with the artsy crowd. He agreed to meet me at three. I finished laundry, did some grocery shopping and wrapped up a few other Saturday chores.

Leland was sitting near the door reading a newspaper when I arrived a few minutes after three. The coffeehouse was rather empty, given its reputed popularity.

"Sorry I'm late," I said taking the other chair at the small table. Shostakovich strings filled the air and the canvases of an apparently demented artist covered the walls.

"I didn't even notice," he said. "I've been reading."

"How's the world of international finance?"

"As dull as ever. How's the world of anthropology?"

"I love it," I said.

He looked at me seriously. "I envy you. You're one of the few people I know who's actually doing what he really wants to do. Most people get caught up in things they hate and don't know how to get out of them." He paused. "Like me."

"I thought you liked the finance game."

"It has its moments. But I wasn't thinking about finance. I was thinking about what's waiting for me in Singapore. It's coming down to the wire. My father wants me to return in September. He's expanding the firm and needs me to help out. They've also decided it's time for me to marry."

"Does Rod fit into any of this?"

He became quiet. "He can't understand that I've got to go back. I want him to come with me, but he won't even consider it."

"He told me," I said. "It's hardly the ideal arrangement."

"We could work something out. After I have a kid, they'll leave me alone and let me do what I want. Rod and I could live together. Maybe I can eventually talk them into letting me open a branch in San Francisco. I'm only asking him to do it for a short time."

"He's coming from a very different place. He can't understand this obligation to your family that you feel above him."

"It's not that way. I don't love my family more than I love him. I'm beginning to resent them for making me go back. I'd do anything for Rod."

"Except not go back to your family."

He looked at me quietly. "You don't understand either."

"I'm trying to tell you how Rod sees it. I don't pretend to be an expert on Chinese culture, but I've been around it enough to appreciate the strong sense of family obligation you have."

"You hit it right on the head," he said. "Why can't Rod see it the way you do?"

"He's in love with you. I'm not."

"I can't bear the thought of being without him."

"Maybe you should try a trial separation. Go back and see if you can work something out with your family. Tell them you're gay. Maybe they'll take it better than you think."

"You don't know my parents. They want a grandson from me, preferably several. Even if I told them I was gay, they would still insist on that."

"Go back and have a son, and then come back to Rod. Maybe he's willing to wait for you."

"It's not that simple. There's the matter of the family business. I'll have to be in Singapore several years to see it through the expansion we're doing."

"I don't see where you have a lot of choice. It's either chuck the family thing and stay with Rod or go back to

Singapore and forget about Rod. I don't think he'll ever go there and live the way you want him to. Not many men would. I certainly wouldn't."

Leland returned to Singapore and Rod remained in San Francisco. Rod gave up their flat shortly after Leland left and rented a small apartment in the Castro. I received a Christmas card from Leland with a long letter telling me how much he hated Singapore and how much he loved Rod. He had called and written Rod but he refused to take the calls and didn't answer the letters. Leland was dreading his marriage which was arranged by his family for the following April. I answered his letter, but didn't hear from him until the following Christmas when I received a card with printed names of him and his wife. There was no note.

For several years, Christmas cards arrived from Leland. In two successive years, two sons' names were added to the card. About the fifth Christmas I didn't receive a card from him and the next year, I cut him from my list.

I occasionally ran into Rod, but I never asked him about Leland. Sometimes he was alone, sometimes with a friend and sometimes with an obvious boyfriend. About four years after they broke up, he moved to Chicago with a lover. I never saw him again.

About eighteen years after Leland left San Francisco, I visited Singapore. I had finished several months of field-work in the southern Philippines and went to Singapore to meet my partner Matt who was flying in from San

Francisco to join me. We planned to spend some time in Burma and then fly to Paris for a few weeks. I was staying at the Raffles Hotel and realizing that I preferred the old, slightly sleazy Raffles to the slick luxurious renovation that was like all the other expensive hotels of the world. I had time on my hands one evening after dinner and was browsing through the telephone directory to see if I could find my surname. As usual, it wasn't listed. I decided to see if Leland was listed. I paged through the formidable list of Wongs and surprisingly found only one Leland. I hesitated for a moment and then dialed the number.

"Hello," said a young man's voice in English.

"May I speak to Leland Wong, please?"

"Just a minute." I heard him shout something in Chinese.

After several moments, a voice said, "Hello."

"Leland, this is a voice from your past. You've probably forgotten me." I identified myself.

"What a surprise," he said. "Of course, I haven't forgotten you. I often think about you. Where are you?"

"At the Raffles. I'm in town for a couple of days and found your name in the phone book. It's been a long time."

"It certainly has been. Almost eighteen years. Are you by yourself?"

"All alone."

"What are you doing tonight?"

"No plans," I said.

"I'll meet you in the Long Bar in half an hour."

"See you there," I said. We hung up.

I put on a fresh shirt and went downstairs. I've always found the Long Bar at the Raffles overrated and disappointing. It's associated with the colorful colonial past of Singapore à la the likes of Maugham, Kipling and Conrad, but every time I've been there it's filled with bored tourists looking for the exotic East. Tonight was no exception, except that it wasn't crowded. I found a table somewhat removed from the others and ordered a harmless drink after refusing a Singapore Sling pushed by the waiter. I checked out the crowd and settled back to wait for Leland. It was a short wait.

I recognized him when he entered the bar, but he was no longer the beautiful young man I remembered from San Francisco. He had gained considerable weight and had that square look that men sometimes acquire in middle age. His hair was still intact but too black. A moustache managed to return some of the character to his face that the weight had taken away. He recognized me and approached my table. I stood and we shook hands.

"You look great," he said. "I would have recognized you anywhere."

"You too," I said.

We made small talk. I told him why I was in Singapore. I asked him about his family. He had two teenage sons.

We were no more than five minutes into the conversation when he asked me, "Do you ever hear anything about Rod?"

"Nothing in years," I said. "The last I heard he moved to Chicago. Have you heard anything?"

"Nothing," he said. "I've tried to make contact over the years, but he never answered my letters."

"So how's life with you? The happily married man?"

"Hardly," he said. "My wife and I don't share the same house. I have a condo downtown where I spend most of my time. She and the boys live at the house. We appear together at the proper functions and then go our separate ways."

"Not an unusual arrangement," I suggested.

"It's a lousy arrangement," he said. "I've resented her since the day I met her. And I resent the boys too. If it weren't for them, I could've been with Rod all these years."

"It's hardly their fault," I said. "You made your own choice."

"I never had a choice in the matter. What I wanted was never important."

"There are always choices. Not always easy. You could've made a different choice." I changed the subject. "Do you have gay friends here?"

"A few. Friends, not lovers. I cruise the parks, the waterfront. Occasionally hit the bars. My taste still runs to vanilla so my choices are limited. Especially as I get older. A few quickies here and there. The rest of the time I keep busy at the office. I often think of the beautiful life Rod and I had in San Francisco. I should never have come back here. How about you? How's your sex life?"

"Rather empty the past few months, but I'm looking forward to seeing my partner tomorrow. We've been together almost twelve years now." I didn't want to dwell on my comfortable domesticity, given Leland's unhappiness with his own.

"Do you ever play around on the side?" he asked with a wink.

"Never felt the need," I said. Leland didn't turn me on when he was young and he turned me on even less now.

He got my message and changed the conversation to Singapore tourist places I might enjoy seeing, most of which didn't remotely interest me. As we talked, he checked out the men in the room. It was apparent that he came to the hotel with the intention of hitting on me. When he discovered I wasn't available, he couldn't wait to leave. After some more small talk that interested neither of us, he said, "Well, it was good seeing you again. I think I'll wander down to the waterfront. Look me up when you're in town again."

We stood and shook hands.

That was the last time I saw Leland Wong.

Her People

IF YOU'RE AN anthropologist, you've heard of Hilda B. Princeton. If you're not, there's little reason why you should know her.

I heard of Hilda B. Princeton many years before I met her at a meeting of the American Anthropological Association in New Orleans where she presented a paper on marriage among the Wutanik, a New Guinea people made famous in anthropology through her writings. After her presentation, I complimented her on what I thought was a good analysis of a complex marriage system. In her mid-fifties, she was tall, thin and severely dressed in tweeds and shoes that could only be called sensible. Her dull brown hair was shingled and small wire-framed glasses encircled her slightly startled pale blue eyes.

"I have read your work with great interest," she told me when she learned my name. "Your people have some interesting affinities to my people."

I've long disliked the "my people" complex of some anthropologists, but it didn't seem the time to tell her so.

"So I've noticed," I said. She was warmly enthusiastic about my research and we chatted about mutual anthropological interests. Her warmth surprised me since she has the reputation of a dragon, competitive and fiercely possessive of "her people." Her position on the grant review board of the National Science Foundation planted the kiss of death on more than one research proposal that came too close to her beloved Wutanik. Probably I was sufficiently removed from "her people" to pose no threat.

During our conversation I discovered that she planned to visit the Wutanik the following summer when I would be traveling in that part of the world. Much to my surprise, she invited me to visit her in the field. Others were eager to talk to her, so I took my leave and told her I hoped we would meet the following summer in New Guinea. She snapped her razor-blade lips into a slash and turned to Dr. Cyril Blanders with whom she has quarreled professionally for the past twenty years, ever since the publication of her now classic monograph *The Significance of Patrilateral Cross-Cousin Marriage and Uxorilocal Residence to Subincision and Clitoridectomy among the Wutanik*. Dr. Blanders' first affront to Hilda B. Princeton was conducting research in a community related to her people. His second, and more fatal, was at a now-legendary meeting when Dr. Blanders questioned the conclusions of Hilda B. Princeton's famous article on the Wutanik penis sheath and its influence on premature ejaculation. In a fit of pique, she whacked Blanders on the head with the penis sheath she used as a visual aid and stomped from the stage. I felt the room heat as

I left them to the next round of their perennial quarrel. Graduate students gathered to take sides.

Now it was late summer and again I found myself in a remote corner of the world, wondering anew about the masochism that makes me forsake creature comforts and seek the backwaters of the earth. This time it was New Guinea and I was on my way to visit Hilda B. Princeton. I planned to stay at the village of her research for a couple of days, and then we would return together to Port Moresby. From there we would travel our separate ways. Despite the heat and the general discomfort of the trip, I was enjoying the adventure. Hilda B. Princeton's writings have insured immortality to the Wutanik within the hallowed halls of anthropology, and an anthropologist's visit to the Wutanik is not unlike a Muslim's pilgrimage to Mecca.

The trip was grueling after leaving Port Moresby. A small plane bounced in like a rubber ball to deposit me at a remote, grass-covered airstrip in the Papuan highlands. From there, I traveled by jeep until the road gave out. At that point Hilda had arranged for two young men from her village to meet me. And now, in their tow, I was on the final leg of my journey. The young men spoke no English, but had an abundance of smiles which they generously shared. The only clothing they wore was their famous penis sheath, a long hollowed dried gourd that encased the penis and attached to a string tied around the waist.

For an hour or so we climbed up and down perpendicular trails, some of the most rugged terrain I've ever encountered. Just as I was beginning to wonder if the trip was worth the effort, we stepped onto a grassy knoll overlooking a lovely valley dotted with small hamlets of thatched houses separated from one another by well-cultivated gardens. The variegated greens of the valley's verdancy blended into the darker greens of the mountain walls which occasionally hosted cascading waterfalls. Above was a dome of blue sky, interrupted only by puffs of white clouds. It was truly a visual feast, and I understood one reason Hilda B. Princeton spent all her free time in this hideaway far from the rest of the world. We began our descent to the valley floor, following a trail worn smooth by the tread of bare feet through unknown centuries.

As we approached a hamlet, we were greeted by a noisy assortment of men, women, children, chickens, pigs and dogs—my introduction to a Wutanik community. They shouted questions to my young guides whose responses soon had the crowd howling with laughter. They stared at me without embarrassment, touched the hair on my arms, felt my beard, explored my boots and marveled at my watch. Not knowing a word of their language, I smiled until my face hurt, hoping I appeared appropriately cordial. The crowd expanded as people came from the gardens to see the stranger the young men had brought to their valley. I looked over their heads for Hilda B. Princeton. Finally, I saw her coming down the main path and breathed a sigh of relief. She cut her way through the crowd, grabbed my hand, gave it an aggressive crunch and said, "So you found my mountain paradise. Welcome to Wutanik land."

I tried not to register surprise, but I was somewhat taken aback. She was wearing only the short fiber skirt worn by Wutanik women, her steel-rimmed glasses and a few beads around her neck. She was bare-footed and bare-breasted. Her flat breasts hung from her bony chest like pockets turned wrong-side out. I smiled, averting my eyes from her peculiar bosom, and said, "Thank you. This is one of the loveliest places I've ever seen."

"Wait until you get to know the people better," she said. "You'll never want to leave."

I heard the splatter of water and looked down to see a child peeing on my boot. As he finished, another wiped her nose on my trouser leg.

"You'll find the children are very uninhibited," said Hilda. "We Americans could learn a lot about child-rearing from these people."

"I'm sure we could," I said, shaking the pee from my boot and feeling my enthusiasm for things Wutanikan wane.

Hilda spoke Wutanikan to the crowd, apparently in response to questions they asked. She then turned to me and said, "I suppose you'll want to get out of those clothes into something native so you won't be so conspicuous. We anthropologists must become native, you know. Otherwise, we can never understand the people we study."

For some time I've wondered if it's possible for any people to ever fully understand another people, whether they go native or whether they're anthropologists. This, however, didn't seem the time to say so. "I brought some shorts," I said.

"I should think you would want to wear the native dress," she said severely, intimating a cancelation of my membership in the American Anthropological Association might be in order.

I looked at the penis sheaths worn by the men standing around us. She looked at my groin appraisingly and said, "I'm sure I can locate something in your size."

"I appreciate your concern," I said, wondering about the sizing system of penis sheaths and thinking Hilda probably had an article about it among her voluminous publications. "But I have very fair skin and I'll get badly sunburned if I strip to a penis sheath. It doesn't seem worth it since I'll be here only a couple of days."

She looked at me with thinly veiled contempt. "Northern Europeans and their deficient pigmentation. Come along and I'll show you your sleeping quarters."

I sighed relief and followed her with the rest of the hamlet to a small thatched hut located centrally in the compound. She crawled through the low door. I followed and soon all the village that could squeeze into the little house joined us. The stifling heat mixed with the various human smells filled the air, but I maintained the smile I'd worn since my arrival.

"You're never alone in Wutanik land," said Hilda. "They're a very gregarious people. You'll never find loneliness here as you do in the United States." Already, I yearned for a bit of that loneliness.

I suddenly felt something prick my thigh and jumped up to discover I had sat on a small arrow. I picked it up as the entire assembly broke into laughter.

"What's so funny?" I asked, trying to remember something Hilda might have written about Wutanik humor, certain that somewhere was such an article.

"The arrow," said Hilda laughing. "You apparently haven't read my article 'Wutanik Courtship and Premarital Sex.' When a man is interested in having sex with a woman, he makes a small arrow and sticks it through the wall of her house. If she is interested in receiving him, she pulls the arrow through the wall. That's his signal to come in for lovemaking. You sat on one of the arrows. Now do you see what's funny?"

I rubbed my thigh, sat down again and tried to look amused.

"A good system, don't you think?" continued Hilda. "Beats ours with all the silly ritual and time our youth go through before they get together."

"I suppose it does simplify matters," I said. "But what if the girl gets an arrow from someone unattractive and unappealing?"

"Another good feature of this culture," she said, and added parenthetically and somewhat reprimandingly, "which you would know if you'd read my article, is that physical beauty is not important in having sex. Sex is a natural drive they fulfill with anyone who's interested. We're too hung up on physical beauty in our culture."

I understood why Hilda might resent that aspect of American culture.

"Leave your backpack here, and I'll give you a tour of the village. I'll wait outside while you change clothes." She turned and crawled through the low door. My eyes averted the bony bare butt exposed by her parted grass skirt.

After hiking half the day, I wasn't too enthusiastic about a walking tour of the village but could think of no gracious way to tell her so. All the villagers remained in the little house, enormously interested in each of my movements. I began unbuttoning my shirt, thinking they might leave if they saw that I intended to undress. Such was not the case, however. When they spotted the hair on my chest, they crowded closer to exclaim and pull at it. It was obvious they weren't going to leave, so I changed into walking shorts as they stared and exclaimed at the anatomical features my disrobing revealed. When I finished, I left the hut and they poured out behind me.

"Ready?" asked Hilda. "I'll show you some households of the village first. Then we'll visit the sweet potato gardens and hike up to the cemetery." She looked at the sun far in the west. "There may not be time for the cemetery today. If not, we'll go tomorrow." She departed at a brisk pace and I hurried to keep up with her, as did the villagers still following us.

"If you recall my monograph *Post-marital Residence and the Role of the Mother's Brother's Affines*, you'll remember that the Wutanik are an uxorilocal-virilineal society, one of the few known in the ethnographic literature. And a greatly misunderstood society, I might add, until I did my research here. You will notice, once you know the people and their kin connections, that all of these households are extended uxorilocal families."

We marched through the village at the aggressive pace she set. Exuding expertise from every pore, she lectured me on the intricacies of the kinship system of the Wutanik, the technology of their house-building, the manufacture of their pottery, the making of fiber skirts, the aesthetics of their art and the nature of their spirits. I felt I should take notes for I was certain she would quiz me later. As we reached the edge of the village, I was relieved when she decided it was too late to visit the sweet potato gardens and the cemetery. She suggested we return to our huts and rest before the evening meal. She accompanied me to my hut and left with a promise of native delicacies for my first Wutanik dinner.

"Of course, you like ethnic food?" she asked, somewhat demandingly.

I assured her I had an adventuresome palate and she left me to my rest. However, most of the village did not. As many people as could crowd into my small hut did so. I was tired of smiling, so I decided to ignore them and settled down to take a short nap. They were totally fascinated, content to sit and watch with great interest my tiniest activity. I closed my eyes and tried to rest while they stared at me, murmuring among themselves. I finally dozed off and when I awakened a half-hour later, they were still staring at me. I wondered again what Hilda B. Princeton found so attractive about these people.

I left my hut to sit in the gathering dusk and wait for Hilda. My Wutanik companions, of course, followed and squatted around me to see what my next move might be.

The heat of the day was diluted by the oncoming night and the first stars appeared in the deepening blue sky. Cooking fires glowed throughout the village as families who were not squatted around me prepared their meals. The accumulated noises of the evening's activities resulted in a not unpleasant din occasionally punctuated by the shouts of children at play. If not for the dozen people sitting within inches of me it would have been a relaxing setting.

I looked down the path and saw Hilda's thin figure determinedly approaching, talking and laughing with people along the way in what seemed flawless Wutanikan. She was obviously very much at home with the people she'd made famous in the world of anthropology. My own research was in a different culture area from Hilda's, and consequently I was not familiar with all her work. I knew, however, that she'd made dozens of field trips to the Wutanik during the past thirty years and because of her prolific publications, they are among the best-documented people in the ethnographic literature. Some of her critics claimed her interpretations were biased by her personal affection for the Wutanik and suggested it might be enlightening to see another anthropologist's interpretations. That, however, seemed unlikely to happen during Hilda Princeton's lifetime. Beyond a few casual visitors like me, she had successfully kept other anthropologists out of Wutanik territory. They were "her people" and she was going to keep them that way.

"So you're up and ready for dinner," said Hilda as she spied me in the evening shadows.

"Pulling at the bit," I said, standing up. "After the hike today, I'm ravenous."

"Good. You're in for some of the best food in New Guinea."

"What are we having for dinner?" I asked.

"I'm not sure. I asked the family of my chief informant to prepare something special. Shall we go?" We set off at her sprinter's pace down the pathway with a small entourage of trotting Wutanik.

We passed several dwellings and entered a large house in the central part of the village, crammed with people of all ages and genders. Several small oil lamps illuminated the room and mats covered the floor. Hilda and I sat while the crowd squatted around us, their dark complexions blending into the dark recesses of the house.

"They're curious about you," she explained. "They don't see many outsiders." She spoke to them and they laughed uproariously. She didn't bother to translate. "See these mats we're sitting on? Some of the best examples of weaving I've ever seen. In fact, you may recognize this one if you read my article 'The Aesthetics of Wutanik Mats and Basketry.' This is one of the illustrations. They have brought it out especially for you."

"I'm afraid I haven't read that article yet," I said, looking at the mat and feeling her reprimand.

I'm a great admirer of non-Western art, but I'm also aware that some people have greater artistic achievements than others. The Wutanik were not such a people. I'd read some of Hilda's papers on Wutanik art and had seen some of the collections she made for various museums. It always seemed to me an interesting kink in New Guinea cultural evolution that the Wutanik should produce such crude art when they were surrounded by people who created some of the finest tribal art in the world. The mat I was examining was an extremely crude specimen, but because it was created by her beloved Wutanik, it was one of the world's great artistic achievements to Hilda Princeton. I examined the coarse mat more closely and began to suspect Hilda had been among the Wutanik too long.

"It is indeed interesting," I said.

She began a short lecture on other Wutanik arts, detailing methods of construction and including brief biographies of some of the more talented artists. She referenced her publications and made appropriate footnotes during her discourse. Each time I asked a question, I felt I should raise my hand.

"Ah, here comes the food," she announced, as two old men pushed their way through the crowd, each carrying two battered pots covered with equally battered, fire-blackened lids. They placed them in front of us.

"You will love this," Hilda said, somewhat dictatorially.

One of the old men shouted something to her and left the house.

"He's gone to get a plate and spoon for you," explained Hilda. "They've heard that white people use plates and spoons, so he's gone for the only plate and spoon in the village. I will, of course, eat the Wutanik way with my hands," she added with obvious superiority.

Within minutes the man was back with a chipped, corroded enamel plate which he placed before me with a rusted spoon speckled with repast remains.

"I really don't mind eating with my hands," I said, not wanting to contaminate the food with the plate and spoon.

"They would be offended if you did so," she said icily. "Use the plate and spoon."

She pulled the pots closer and removed the lids. Various bizarre odors assaulted the room and my appetite plummeted.

"You must try this," she said. She stuck her hand into one of the pots and plopped three moving morsels on my plate. Each was about three inches long, dark green in color and more than anything else looked like the large worms that occasionally attacked tomato plants in my mother's garden.

I was afraid to ask, but I did. "What are they?"

"Grubs. One of the Wutanik delicacies." She took one from the pot, plopped it into her mouth, gave a determined chew and swallowed it. "Just stick it in your mouth. Eat it whole," she said, licking her thin lips like a lizard.

My stomach was churning and moving to my throat as I looked at the worms on my plate. No way could I put those disgusting things in my mouth.

"I hope you like them," said Hilda, ominously. "Two men spent most of the day finding them for you."

I knew I couldn't swallow a whole worm, so I decided to cut one in half. I couldn't have made a worse decision.

When my rusty spoon broke through the skin, green ooze popped out and sprayed the plate.

"That's the best part," said Hilda. "Put the entire worm in your mouth like I told you." I flashed on having to finish my vegetables as a child before I could leave the table. Then I steeled myself against the worms. If Hilda could eat them, so could I. I plopped one of the revolting worms into my mouth, shut off my taste buds and swallowed it.

"Delicious, isn't it?" said Hilda, slurping down another one.

"Delicious," I said, rapidly swallowing two more before my sanity returned.

The other dishes were primarily vegetarian and I didn't ask the details of their ingredients. I did, however, spot the small foot of a gecko floating in the dark brine of a dish that consisted mostly of sweet potato leaves and some kind of grass. I sampled each dish and ate what seemed an appropriate amount.

Hilda, of course, ate with gusto. She stuffed her mouth, licked her fingers and shouted compliments to the cooks. She rhapsodized about the culinary merits of each dish and lamented how she missed the food when she returned home. As I watched her gobble the food, I wondered again about her uncritical acceptance of everything Wutanik.

I finished the meal, having consumed what I considered an appropriate amount, although Hilda intimated that an anthropologist worth his salt would have eaten more enthusiastically and quantitatively. I belied the hunger pains that lurked in my stomach and told her I was a light eater.

After dinner we lounged on mats while the villagers sat watching us, fascinated by our every movement. Hilda slipped into lecture mode and discoursed on the economics of Wutanik agriculture, occasionally quoting from her publications, and emphasizing its superiority to almost every system devised throughout human history. She obviously had found her Shangri-La among the Wutanik. Everything they did was superior to that of all other human societies, especially American society. Hilda concluded the evening with a gigantic cigar made of local, foul-smelling tobacco. She puffed at it with her fellow Wutanikans and filled the house with its vile smoke. When she offered it to me, I declined, saying I was a nonsmoker.

"It's a sign of respect and good manners to smoke with your host," she said, quoting I'm sure, from one of her papers.

"I'm sorry but I'm allergic to smoke. Please explain to them."

"Humph!" she snorted, giving me ten more demerits as an anthropologist. She muttered something in Wutanikan. The people were obviously unconcerned whether or not I smoked. I wondered how well Hilda really knew them.

She conversed with two Wutanik men who shared her cigar as she lounged on the mat with her flat breasts drooping from her bony chest and her skinny legs protruding from the fiber skirt. I contrasted her appearance to the bespectacled, slightly prudish academician who always dressed in proper, tailored tweeds. I tried to imagine her delivering one of her famous papers at an anthropology conference dressed in her present attire. My fantasies were interrupted when she announced it was time to retire.

"Early to bed and early to rise in Wutanik land," she said as she stood up.

She conveyed my thanks to our hosts and with half the company we walked briskly to my hut.

"I must finish several small chores in the morning, so if you want to sleep late, you may," she said, stopping in front of my hut. "Then I'll show you the rest of the community. Tomorrow night the village is having a farewell party for me. There'll be lots of food and dancing. I'm sure you'll enjoy it. I'll stop by about nine in the morning. It's improper for a guest to sleep alone so these two men will sleep with you." She turned and left.

I would have preferred solitary sleep, but two companions were certainly preferable to the crowd that had surrounded me since my arrival. I smiled at my companions and we entered the hut. After finding a comfortable spot on the lumpy floor, I fell asleep immediately and slept soundly until the noises of the village awakened me shortly after sunrise.

True to her word, Hilda appeared punctually at nine o'clock. She brought a breakfast of cold sweet potatoes and a fruit she assured me was exotic, but tasted of alum and sugar water. I ate heartily of the cold, baked sweet potatoes. They were bland, but harmless, and managed to fill the empty caverns of my stomach. She congratulated me on my appreciation of Wutanik food and told me to eat plenty since we would not eat again until evening.

"I hope I'm not interfering with any work you want to do your last day here," I said.

"Of course not," she assured me. "I planned to spend today showing you the community. Besides I always spend my last day visiting friends and taking a farewell look at things. Are you ready?"

I replied that I was and we set off at her rapid pace. She gave me an extensive tour of the community where she had spent most of her vacations, sabbaticals and leaves during the past thirty years. The day amounted to a marathon lecture on the Wutanik. Occasionally I would ask a question that bordered on her personal life. I usually received a monosyllabic answer and she immediately returned to some esoteric aspect of Wutanik culture. She was obviously not interested in talking about herself and as the day wore on, I began to realize that the Wutanik were Hilda Princeton's chief *raison d'être*.

As she eulogized the merits of everything Wutanikan, I tried to view what I saw and heard through more objective lenses. I personally found the Wutanik rather uninteresting as a culture. I well know the anthropological dictum of cultural relativity that all cultures are legitimate expressions of the human experience and no culture is superior or inferior to another. But when I abandoned my anthropological robes and donned my personal garb, I found the Wutanik lacking in a good many things I find attractive in human cultures. Their social and political organization seemed repressive to me. Demons and spirits that frightened and cajoled people into following their sometimes cruel dictates dominated their religious life. Their art was crude, static and unimaginative. Their food—I think I've made myself clear on that one. They conducted periodic raids on their neighbors that persisted until a victim was slain, at which time the neighbors then raided their villages with murder in mind. Their oral traditions were limited to a few obscene riddles and stories about malevolent spirits. Taking advantage of the frailties of a fellow Wutanik was the basis of most of their humor. In short, they were not my kind of people.

But they were obviously Hilda Princeton's kind of people. Accolades preceded everything she had to say about "her people." We visited several small hamlets, entered households to observe the daily chores of living, watched women work in their sweet potato gardens, witnessed a pig-butchering, saw a shaman exorcise a spirit, climbed a mountainside to visit a cemetery and played with children at their games. As much as possible within the span of six hours, I saw the gamut of Wutanik life.

As we approached my hut, I expressed my gratitude to Hilda for taking the time to show me the community she knew so well. She replied that she always enjoyed talking about the Wutanik and was happy to share her knowledge with me. She parted with a promise to return at six o'clock and escort me to the farewell feast that evening. I went into the hut for the first time by myself and pondered this strange woman who found such happiness here.

*   *   *

Predictably, Hilda arrived punctually. A bright red flower perched precariously atop her head, she was in high spirits and assured me that tonight's events would be the highlight of my short stay among the Wutanik.

We walked to the same house where we'd had dinner the previous evening, but this time we remained outdoors where most of the village was gathered. The central area of the compound was empty, but people milled around the edges, talking loudly and excitedly. A group of bored-looking musicians sat at one side beating monotonously on drums made of hollow logs. Children scurried about with their noisy, rough games. We approached a group of men in charge of cooking. Hilda joked with them and we left them laughing hilariously. She stopped to chat with some dour-looking crones who broke into broad smiles before our departure. Children ran to Hilda and she joined some of their games. We finally arrived at a spot in the compound that was prepared especially for us. We sat on mats and watched the activities around us while Hilda continued her lecture series on Wutanik culture.

"You'll enjoy the dances," she announced. "They are the highest expression of Wutanik aesthetics, so subtle in their execution that it takes a sensitive eye to appreciate them."

I hoped I had such an eye, but suspected otherwise since so many of the merits of Wutanik culture Hilda pointed out totally escaped me.

"We'll eat first and then the dancing will begin. You may want to join them."

I doubted that I would, and hoped I wouldn't have to.

"Ah, here comes the food." My eyes followed Hilda's to four men crossing the open area before us with fire-blackened pots.

"You'll notice," she began in the pontifical tones that usually preceded one of her lectures, "that pots and knives are the only trade items these people use. When I first came here, they were still using stone blades for knives and clay pots for cooking. I tried to discourage them from abandoning them, but didn't have much luck. I hope I don't live to see these people defiled by the West."

Since I first arrived in the village, it was apparent that Hilda Princeton was of the anthropological school that believes tribal people should be retained as museum pieces, living in isolated enclaves protected from the modern world. It was another view we didn't share, so I made no comment and began to examine with some apprehension the dishes placed before us.

Hilda continued. "The Wutanik utilize every food source in their environment. Everything that is edible is eaten by them."

That did nothing for my appetite.

"I won't tell you the ingredients of the dishes until you've tried them," she announced. "Americans have such cultural hang-ups about food that I'm sure you wouldn't taste some of the dishes if you knew the ingredients." She discoursed on the inflexibility of the American palate. Like many anthropologists, she was tolerant of all cultures except her own.

"Try this," she said. She plopped a piece of unsavory-looking meat on the old enamel plate that had resurrected for my use. The meat was anemic gray and its butchers were unsuccessful in removing all the hair from its anonymous carcass. Without dwelling on the possible identity of the unappetizing flesh before me, I stuck it in my mouth and swallowed without chewing. Hilda followed suit but chewed hers long and leisurely.

"Not bad, eh?" she said, taking a second piece. "It always reminds me of rabbit. Do you know what it is?"

"No," I said, and then with some hesitation, "What is it?"

"Rat," said Hilda. "The countryside abounds with them and they would be a nuisance if the Wutanik didn't utilize them for food. Think how we could eliminate the rat problems in our cities—not to mention the entire world—if we could convince people that they are a legitimate food source. I'm working on a paper to that effect which I'll present at the American Anthropological Association meeting next fall. The Wutanik have so much to teach the world. Want another piece?"

I shook my head greenly, saying I wanted to save room for the other dishes. Few animals revolt me more than rats and several of them found their way into the evening's meal. Among the surprises that Hilda and the Wutanik had in store for me included bat cooked with sweet potato leaves and snake roasted in an underground oven and served in a coil. As I tasted each dish, I waited nervously for Hilda to announce what I'd just eaten. And, in all fairness, I must admit that some of them were rather tasty. The baked sweet potatoes were good, as was a pudding made of sweet potatoes and sugar cane. The roast pig was succulent. Unfortunately, my appreciation for the tasty dishes was considerably dampened by the less appetizing concoctions. I ate what I could stomach and stuffed what I couldn't into my pockets when Hilda and the Wutanik weren't watching. Finally, Hilda announced she was finished and the dishes were cleared away. I stretched out in relief to enjoy the dances which Hilda promised would soon begin.

The monotonous wooden drums sounded throughout dinner. Now the drummers were joined by three men who blew flute-like instruments that pierced the night and seemed totally indifferent to what the drummers were doing. About twelve men lined up on one side of the open space and directly across from them was an equal number of women. They glared at one another fiercely and then began movements that I soon learned were the extent of Wutanik choreography. Each line jutted out left hips at the opposite line. Left hands were placed on the hips while right hands were held above the heads. The little fingers of the raised hands were flipped back and forth to the beat of the drums. After about five minutes, the entire group switched hips and flipped their little fingers again. Several minutes later, they returned to their original positions. Such was the nature of Wutanik dance.

"The subtle grace," sighed Hilda.

I looked at her and then back at the dancers. I saw neither subtlety nor grace.

Suddenly, Hilda whinnied and trotted to the center of the dance arena. She struck the stance of the dancers and wiggled her little fingers to the beat of the drums with a look of ecstasy on her face. The crowd cheered her efforts. Several Wutanik men near me gestured that I should join her. I declined but they persisted, practically dragging me to Hilda's side. I felt like a perfect fool as I tried to imitate the movements of the dance. I thrust my hip and wiggled my little fingers for about five minutes and then sat down. Hilda was oblivious to everything, yielding to the sounds and movements of the dance as her peculiar breasts flapped to the beat of the drums. Finally, after about a half-hour of the monotonous dances, the musicians stopped and Hilda returned to my side.

"Now that is pure art," she said arranging herself beside me.

The next stage of the evening was ushered in with an enormous pot of gurgling liquor placed before us by three grimy old men.

"This is Wutanik beer," announced Hilda, followed by what I could now predict: "It is far superior to anything we call beer."

She dipped a clay cup into the pot and handed it to me. She filled another cup for herself and proposed a toast. "To the Wutanik. May they lead the world out of its insanity." We touched cups and drank.

If kerosene were mixed with chili peppers and rotted sweet potatoes and allowed to ferment for a month, the taste might approximate the beer of the Wutanik. I gagged and spit out the evil brew, much to the delight of the crowd eagerly awaiting my reaction.

"I'm afraid it's not my kind of drink," I said to Hilda who was laughing loudly and guzzling from her clay cup.

"Don't worry," she said. "It took me a while to get used to it. Once you acquire a taste for it, you won't be able to live without it."

I doubted that very much.

For the rest of the evening, the entire crowd—men, women and children—drank generously of the local brew. Before long, everyone was in some state of intoxication, including Hilda who drank incredible amounts of the liquor. She spoke to me only in Wutanikan as she joked and shouted to the people around her. Everyone was having a grand time. I smiled and sipped at the cup gurgling in my hand. Hilda was totally involved with her Wutanik friends, laughing hilariously and joining them in impromptu, obscene dances. I was soon forgotten by everyone, so after about a half-hour of watching the festivities, I slipped back to my hut.

I sat outside watching the stars above, listening to the sounds of the celebration down the path and wondering what strange kink in Hilda found this society so attractive. Finally, exhaustion overtook me and I crawled inside to sleep a dreamless sleep.

I awakened early the next morning. I packed my backpack and walked to Hilda's little house. She was efficiently packing her surprisingly few possessions into a backpack. She had abandoned her Wutanik costume and was dressed in walking boots, trousers, shirt and a solar topee.

"I'm almost ready," she announced. "It'll take about four hours to reach the mission station where we'll spend the night. Did you enjoy the party last night?"

"It was very interesting," I said, wondering how many times I'd used that innocuous adjective since arriving.

In her hand was a small arrow, the size of the one I sat on my first day in the village. She wrote something on its shaft and turned to rummage in her backpack. "Let me finish this and I'll be ready to go," she said.

I glanced at the writing on the arrow shaft. It was a name, followed by last night's date. She retrieved a small bundle of arrows from her backpack. She slipped the loose arrow into the bundle, gave it a solid pat and held it to her bosom with a happy sigh.

"It's always so difficult for me to leave," she said, smiling down at the arrows. "But I'll be back at Christmas." She returned the arrows to her backpack and said, "Let's go."

A quiet smile overtook my face.

We left the house, strapped on our backpacks and walked through the village, waving goodbye to the villagers. When we reached the mountain trail, I was still smiling. I now understood one of the reasons Hilda B. Princeton was so enamored of the Wutanik.

Doing Asia

I FIRST SAW THEM in Bangkok at the Oriental Hotel. I was enjoying the luxury of that beautiful old hotel while recuperating from an exhausting visit to a colleague who was doing archeology in the remote hills of northern Thailand. I savored a late breakfast on the verandah overlooking the Chao Phraya River while watching the never-ending parade of watery traffic moving up and down that muddy stream. After several trips to Asia on a student budget, I was traveling tourist-class to see if Asia looked any different from that perspective. If nothing else, the food and beds were better and the hotels I stayed in didn't turn into brothels after midnight—or if they did, they were more discreet about it.

They sat at the table beside me. They looked like any number of middle-aged white American couples traveling in Asia in the late 1970s. The man was portly and polyestered with a florid face and thinning, gray hair. The woman was powdered and plump with hair tinted an attractive soft blond.

"This awful hot weather," she complained, wiping her forehead with a small lavender handkerchief. "How do these natives stand it?"

"Feels good after that air conditioner inside," said her husband. "I almost froze to death last night."

"Smell that river?" asked his wife, covering her nose with her handkerchief and making a face. "Some of these smells make me ill." She shuddered slightly.

"What are you going to have?" asked her husband, scanning the menu.

"Anything but Thai food." She pronounced Thai as she would the upper anatomy of her leg. "That food last night was terrible. I had indigestion all night long. I don't know how they eat such spicy food."

"They use spices to cover up the taste. Who knows what goes into the pot in the kitchen?"

"I'm going to have the American breakfast," said the wife.

"Only God knows what that'll be. When you order be sure you point at what you want. None of these waiters understand English. You'd think that would be required for working here."

"There's a silk shop I want to visit today," said the woman, setting her menu aside. "Hazel Thornton told me about it. She said the colors are like American colors, not so garish as Thai colors. I might have a dress made if I see something I like."

A smiling waiter approached to take their orders. They pointed to the menu, speaking loudly, as if by doing so he would better understand English.

"He seemed to understand," said the wife after the waiter left.

"They always *seem* to understand. They smile and shake their heads and then bring you something totally different from what you ordered. I'll be glad to get someplace where they speak American English."

The woman looked around the verandah, spotted me, smiled and said, "Good morning." I returned her greeting, hurriedly finished my coffee, and left before she could begin a conversation.

Two days later I departed Bangkok for Burma where I spent a few days in Pagan, the spectacular site in central Burma famous for its thousands of pagodas. I returned to my small hotel late one afternoon after a day of sightseeing and was sitting on the deck overlooking the meandering Irrawaddy River. As I enjoyed the mellow mood of the evening, I heard a familiar voice behind me. It was the woman I'd seen at the Oriental Hotel in Bangkok. She and her husband were settling into chairs near me. Both looked tired, rumpled and disgruntled.

"I don't know why we came all this way to see a bunch of crumbling buildings," said the husband, wiping his large red face with a soiled white handkerchief. "They aren't all that different from the ones in Bangkok."

"Everyone who comes to Burma has to see Pagan," said his wife. "And besides we found some nice lacquerware."

"Probably could've bought it cheaper in L.A."

A waiter placed two bottles of beer before them, smiled and left.

The man poured a glassful and took a drink. "Tastes like piss," he said, making a face. "I haven't had good beer since we left Tokyo."

"It's horrible," said his wife after sampling hers. She looked out over the Irrawaddy. "But you must admit the hotel is nice, especially after the one we had in Rangoon."

"I'm going to write the Burmese government about that Rangoon rat-trap. I wouldn't be caught dead in such a dump in America."

"Sometimes I wish we didn't have to go to Mandalay," sighed his wife. "The Thorntons said the hotel isn't too good there."

"Who says we *have* to go to Mandalay?"

"Whoever heard of coming to Burma and not going to Mandalay?" asked his wife, reproachfully. "The Thorntons said it's a lovely city."

"Yeah, and they said Manila, Bangkok, Rangoon and Pagan were lovely. If we've seen the lovely parts of Asia, I can't imagine what the bad parts are like."

"This heat is unbearable." The wife fanned herself with her handkerchief. "I don't know how the natives work in it."

"Most of them don't. That's the problem with these hot countries. No one works and nothing gets done."

I decided against a second drink and walked down to the river before they recognized me.

I left Pagan the following day and three days later flew to India. I planned to bypass Calcutta which perhaps epitomizes the urban ills of the world, and fly straight to Delhi where I would tour northern India before going on to Karachi. However, mechanical problems forced the plane down at Calcutta.

We arrived late afternoon and were informed we wouldn't leave until eleven that night. I finished my only book and couldn't find a newsstand where I might buy another. I was bored with the delay and tired of the crowded airport. The seats in the lounge couldn't accommodate all of the delayed multicultural passengers who were scattered over the floor and atop closed ticket counters, window sills and planter boxes. Magnificently bearded Sikh men with colorful turbans wandered throughout the crowd. A group of Saudi Arabian men in white robes carried on a heated, aggressive conversation while their women, totally covered in dark purdah, clustered noiselessly aside. Hindu women in brilliant saris floated around the room like exotic butterflies occasionally alighting on a vacated seat. The conservative dark suits of Japanese businessmen added a somber note to the assembly while a scattering of chalky European faces appeared as alien apparitions. Standing at the far end of the lounge, three Buddhist monks in saffron robes quietly discussed matters possibly spiritual.

As I surveyed the crowd, I was surprised to see the American couple I seemed to be following throughout Asia sitting alone and looking extremely weary, unhappy and apprehensive.

I wandered over to the Air India counter and learned the plane was delayed an additional three hours. We would not leave until two in the morning. My feet were tired, so I looked for a place to sit. The only available space was beside the American couple who were now dozing. When I sat beside the woman, she awakened with a start and clutched her purse.

"I'm sorry," I said. "I didn't mean to frighten you."

"That's alright," she smiled, moving to give me additional space. She apparently didn't recognize me from our other brief encounters. "Are you on the flight to Delhi?" she asked.

"Yes. I'm afraid it's been delayed again. Now they say it won't leave until one o'clock."

"One o'clock!" moaned her husband, awakened by our conversation. "Damn! This'll be our one and only trip to Asia. I've never seen such a backward place. Worse than South America. We'll be lucky if we get out of here tomorrow morning."

"Probably we won't," said his wife, gloomily. "They'll keep delaying the departure by an hour or two so they won't have to put us up in a hotel. Not that I would sleep in a hotel in this city." She turned to me. "Friends of ours were here and advised us to bypass Calcutta. They said it's terribly dirty, and the beggars and hordes of people are awful. We planned to go straight to Delhi."

Her husband thrust a beefy hand at me and said, "I'm Oliver Breen. This is my wife Evelyn." I shook hands and told them my name.

"Is this your first trip to Asia?" asked Breen.

"No. I've traveled in Asia before."

"You have?" he asked incredulously. "You mean you've been here before and you came back? I can't imagine why."

"Now, Oliver. There are some pretty things to see here. You liked the palace in Bangkok."

"Would've been a hell of a lot easier and cheaper to see it on video back in L.A."

"Do you think they'll serve us something to eat?" asked Mrs. Breen.

"You won't catch me eating anything here," said her husband. "I'm not eating until we get to an American hotel. I've had enough foreign food."

"Do you travel often?" I asked, thinking their provincialism must reflect limited travel.

"Oh yes," said Mrs. Breen. "Each year we take a trip. We've seen most of the world. This year we're doing Asia. We were never attracted to Asia until last year when some of our friends visited here. We decided to come over after hearing their stories."

"You'll never catch me here again," muttered Breen.

"Oliver's had trouble with the food and water," said his wife, puckering her plump face into a sympathetic little frown.

"Been shittin' like a goose since we left Japan. This is the filthiest place I've ever seen."

"Now Oliver, the trip hasn't been all bad. We've bought some lovely things. And some of the hotels have been nice. That one in Manila was just like home. Everyone spoke such good English."

"Just like home until you stepped out the front door and took a sniff. The entire city smelled like a toilet. And what have you bought here that you couldn't buy at home? You can buy anything you want in Los Angeles—at least, anything that's worth buying." He looked around the room. "Look at this filthy airport. Can you imagine an international airport in this shape back home? You should see the one in Rangoon. The worst mistake these countries ever made was getting rid of the whites. They've gone downhill ever since the whites left. God knows though, I can understand why they wanted to leave."

"I don't think they exactly wanted to leave," I said, remembering the various battles throughout Asia that finally ousted the colonial powers.

He glanced at me unpleasantly and directed his attention to an Indian family spreading mats on the floor several feet away. I noticed a newsmagazine on Mrs. Breen's lap.

"May I borrow your magazine? I've run out of reading material."

"Of course," she said, handing it to me. I began reading and when I finished the magazine, the Breens were dozing again, so I placed it on the seat and wandered around the lounge.

The public address system crackled and with everyone else in the lounge, I awaited a voice. It spoke in Hindi, a rather long announcement that brought groans from those who understood it. Then a shorter English translation followed: "Ladies and gentlemen, we regret that Air India Flight 176 to Delhi has been further delayed until nine o'clock tomorrow morning. We have found accommodations at the Grand Hotel in Calcutta for all passengers. Buses will provide transportation to the hotel. We regret the delay and appreciate your patience. Thank you."

I groaned with the rest of the crowd. While contemplating my next move, I saw the Breens approaching me.

"Are you going into Calcutta?" asked Breen.

"Seems better than staying here all night."

"From what I've heard, it's terrible," said Mrs. Breen, her face a frightened frown. "I don't trust the hotels in this city."

"I'm sure they'll put us up at a comfortable place," I said.

"Maybe we should go in, Oliver. It can't be worse than staying here at this awful airport." Mrs. Breen looked at her husband pleadingly.

He sighed in exasperation. "If you insist. But remember, everyone warned us about Calcutta."

"One night in a hotel can't be that bad," said his wife, looking at me for affirmation.

"I'm sure it'll be alright," I said.

A large bus, driven by a turquoise-turbaned Sikh, growled to a halt outside the terminal lounge. Two others pulled up behind it. The restless passengers pushed through the lounge exit into the warm tropical night where an attractive Indian flight attendant checked our names on a list.

"How long will we be at the hotel?" Breen asked the attendant.

"The flight departs tomorrow morning at nine, but we'll leave the hotel at seven," she replied with a professional smile.

"Hardly worth going in," grumbled Breen, following his wife into the bus. She sat at a window and he took the seat beside her. I sat at the window seat behind them.

When the bus was filled, the driver ground it into gear and slowly drove into the night.

We departed the airport and turned onto the congested highway to Calcutta. Bullocks lumbered to the sides of the road, dragging two-wheeled carts crammed with people and their belongings. We honked our way past them. As we approached Calcutta, traffic thickened and the small shacks along the highway yielded to more substantial buildings. The sidewalks and roadsides appeared littered with colorful bundles which I soon realized were sleeping people, part of the infamous millions who live on the Calcutta streets. Some gathered in doorways, others lay alongside buildings while still others slept together in walkways. Occasional small fires illuminated families preparing food.

In front of me Mrs. Breen murmured, "Oh, Oliver. They must be those poor people the Thorntons told us about. They're living on the streets."

Her husband leaned over, peered out the window and muttered, "Damn shame."

As we drove deeper into Calcutta, the driver sounded his horn repeatedly to ease his way through the crowded road. People spilled from sidewalks onto the road, standing and squatting in small groups, ignoring the lights and horn of the bus.

I heard Mrs. Breen murmur softly, "I never dreamed it was so bad."

Her husband added, "Damn shame people have to live this way. Damn shame."

The crowd became denser as we crept into the city, the driver honking his horn and inching his way through the human sea. Occasionally we came to a standstill, waiting for people to make room for our passage. A face or two looked up at the bus, but for the most part we were ignored until we came to a complete halt and the driver leaned on the horn. Sleeping people awakened. Some saw the bus filled with foreigners and crammed against the sides, thrusting up hands for money. A young mother shoved an infant, grotesquely deformed by a harelip, against the window where Mrs. Breen was sitting. She screamed for money and beat on the glass. A man beside her with stubs for hands pounded my window.

"Oh, Oliver, I can't stand it," cried Mrs. Breen. She looked away from the window.

"Now Evelyn," said her husband. "Damn shame."

Emaciated children with swollen stomachs and skin diseases were held up to our windows with shouts for money. Adults held fingers to mouths conveying their hunger. Finally, the bus pulled away from the crowd and we gained a modicum of speed as we moved through the street. Soon we came to a halt. Outside, a large neon sign announced the Grand Hotel, our destination. When we stepped from the bus, a woman, dressed in rags, spotted Mrs. Breen. She ran to her and shoved a nude infant toward her. The child was dead. Mrs. Breen screamed as the woman stretched out her arm demanding money. Breen sheltered his wife, pushing through the mob toward the hotel. The woman then thrust the dead child at me. An ancient man, his face eaten by some horrible disease, blocked the Breens' path, waving a pan for money. A young man with no eyes led by an old woman also demanded alms. Children, blackened with grime and dwarfed by malnutrition, tugged at our garments.

We squeezed through the press of poverty and disease and finally reached the lobby of the hotel. Mrs. Breen was sobbing. Her husband, very shaken, comforted her as they sat on a sofa. I fell into an armchair. A crystal chandelier at least six feet in diameter hung above me. Oriental carpets covered the marble floors and tooled leather furniture provided seating throughout. Brilliant bouquets added splashes of color that complemented the tapestries adorning the walls. Uniformed in white, the hotel staff circulated among the arriving guests with cool beverages.

The Breens approached and asked if I knew what was happening. They appeared shaken and lost.

"I think we're supposed to get room assignments at the desk," I said.

"Those poor, miserable people," said Mrs. Breen, sadly. "I knew India was poor, but I never dreamed . . ."

"Now, Evelyn," said her husband.

"And we complain about our conditions at home," she continued. "Our poorest are better off than these people. And most of us live like royalty. I'll never complain again. We are so spoiled. Those poor, poor people."

She cried softly into her handkerchief.

"Wait here," I suggested to the Breens. "Give me your airline tickets and I'll get your room assignment."

I walked to the reservation desk and waited for the impatient crowd to subside. Finally, it thinned and I was given room assignments. I told the Breens their room number and gave them their key. They thanked me, walked across the lobby and disappeared into an elevator.

Unready for sleep, I went to the bar for a drink. However, once inside the crowded noisy room, I decided against the drink when I noticed a door leading to an inner courtyard. I went outside and sat in a chair overlooking a fountain of tumbling water. I don't know how long I sat there, reliving the ride through Calcutta. Finally I left, found my room and crawled into bed. But no sleep came as I tossed, haunted by that midnight ride and remembering I had to repeat it in the morning. I kept telling myself that the people who approached us were the most desperate of the lot, using their physical deformities to gain our sympathies and money. But it did no good. Those uninterested in us led lives of equal squalor.

As the room lightened with dawn, I finally fell asleep. Within minutes, however, I was awakened by a telephone telling me the buses would leave for the airport in an hour. I stumbled into the shower and cleared my numb head with cold water. Then I went downstairs to face breakfast and the return ride to the airport.

The breakfast room was sumptuous. It opened onto a garden riotous with brilliant bougainvillea and studded with stately palms. Caged parrots scattered throughout the room added their chatter and color to the noises of the diners. White wicker furniture upholstered in cool mint green provided seating. I watched heaping plates of food served, much of it returned uneaten to the kitchen as garbage. I ordered tea and toast, consumed it without tasting it, and left the dining room to wait in the lobby.

The Breens entered and sat beside me. They looked exhausted. Mrs. Breen smiled wanly and said, "I didn't sleep much. I kept thinking of those poor people outside and how awful we've been on this trip. All we've done is complain because everything is not like we have it at home. We have so much. We have no right to ever complain again." She pulled her handkerchief from her purse and dabbed her eyes.

"Now, Evelyn," said her husband. "You're exhausted. You must try to forget it."

"I'll never forget it," she sniffled. "Never. I shall never forget that poor woman and her dead baby." She cried into her handkerchief.

"Do you know when the bus is leaving?" asked Breen, obviously trying to change the subject.

"I think at seven," I said. "People are lining up at the door. Perhaps we should join them."

We joined the line and within minutes it began moving toward the waiting busses. Beggars surrounded the entrance, but hotel employees were stationed to keep them from approaching us. Most passengers chose to look down or straight ahead to avoid the eyes of the pressing crowd. We entered the bus and again I found myself at a window seat, this time directly in front of the Breens.

The streets were even more congested than the night before. The bus crept as people and cattle eased out of its way. My travels in other parts of Asia had not prepared me for Calcutta. Never had I seen so many people living in such poverty under such degrading conditions. People were obviously cheaper than beasts of burden; they, rather than animals, pulled heavy wooden-wheeled carts piled with precarious loads. Two small men, their sinews tearing at their bones, struggled to get their cart from the path of the bus. Men and boys, wearing only ragged shorts, pulled rickshaws through the mob. At a construction site, women and girls tugging at ropes and prying with poles moved heavy stones. Some people slept on the sidewalks while others prepared food at fires fed by cow dung. Cattle roamed freely, their bony ribs brushing through the crowd.

Each time the bus stopped, people pawed at the windows, crying for money or food. Occasionally angered when nothing was forthcoming, they beat at the windows and the sides of the bus. Several passengers chose to read, rather than watch the people of the streets. Others looked stonily ahead. A young French woman, dressed in the faded denim of her peers, became angered at the demanding people beyond her window and covered it with a scarf. Beside me, an Indian man quietly read the morning newspaper. The driver lay on his horn to part a path through the flood of people. The squalor spread in all directions like a cancer run wild.

Finally, the bus pulled off the crowded street and entered the main thoroughfare to the airport. We moved faster now, but the road was only slightly less crowded. Buildings were fewer, but all space was filled with hovels constructed of rags, cardboard and scraps of wood stretching endlessly as far as I could see. It seemed the aftermath of some great disaster. As indeed it was.

A huge sign at the road entering the airport read: "The East is Eden. India." Beneath it, people slept with ragged bundles. When I stepped from the bus at the airport, a boy without legs begged for coins. Inside the terminal, Mrs. Breen turned to me and announced, "This has been a message from God. He has shown me the poverty and sickness of the world because I didn't appreciate the goodness of my life. God has been so good to me. I've seen his light. I shall never complain again. I have been so selfish."

I offered a secular response and was soon separated from the Breens by the passengers pressing around the check-in counter. I made it through airport security and finally found myself on the long-delayed flight. I didn't see the Breens when I deplaned at Delhi and assumed I would never see them again.

I spent the next two weeks touring India. The country was all I expected and much more. Probably the human spirit has never reached greater heights or greater lows than in India. I marveled at the awesome temples carved in stone caves at Ajanta and Ellora, and wept inwardly for the wretched poor begging for food while awaiting death on the streets of the sprawling urban disasters. The quiet, majestic purity of the Taj Mahal moved me to aesthetic heights I've seldom experienced while the cremation ceremonies on the ghats of the Ganges at Varanasi taught me more about spirituality than all the books I've ever read. All one has read of India is there, and much more. Never have I been so aesthetically moved or so emotionally disturbed as I was by India. Thus, I left both eagerly and reluctantly.

*　　*　　*

Karachi was my next stop.

By no stretch of the imagination can Karachi be called beautiful, fascinating, but not beautiful. It sprawls unattractively in all directions in a natural setting that was probably already unremarkable before the urban sprawl consumed it. But its people give Karachi vibrancy. A stroll through the heart of the old city revealed women in purdah viewing the world through small peek-holes, camels pulling ancient wooden-wheeled carts, snake-charmers playing melancholy tunes to shimmering serpents, shops of colorful hand-knotted carpets, turbans and head gear of every imaginable size, shape, texture and color, a potpourri of racial types that would delight any anthropologist, the disabled and the destitute begging for coins, beards running the gamut of beard possibilities—bicycles, motor scooters, trucks, jeeps, carts and busses painted in every imaginable color, honking and beeping through the packed thoroughfares.

I could easily have disappeared into this colorful mayhem, but fortunately a friend from graduate school days, took me in tow and showed me the sights of her city. After touring Karachi, we visited some of the prehistoric sites of the Indus Valley where I gained a greater appreciation for those ancient cultures.

My last night in Karachi, we dined on the top floor of the tallest building in the city. It was a delicious dinner of Pakistani cuisine and the evening was a pleasant one. With the lights of the city scattered around us like an inverted starry sky, we caught up on the details of our lives since we last met. After dessert, my friend asked me to accompany her to the other side of the room so she could point out landmarks of the city. We stood at the windows and I followed her hands as she familiarized me with the layout of her hometown. I slowly became aware of voices behind us.

"Wipe the utensils with your napkin," said a man. "This may be an American hotel, but you know who's working in the kitchen."

"This food is absolutely awful," grumbled a woman. "If they advertise American food, they should prepare it properly."

"What do you expect in this country? There was nothing else on the menu but that Pakistan stuff. I'd starve before I ate that."

"Considering the price we paid for this champagne, you'd expect it to be drinkable," complained the woman. "Tomorrow we'll buy our carpets and get out of this filthy place."

I turned slightly to glance at the couple. Mr. Breen was digging irritably into the heaping plate of food before him while Mrs. Breen peered unpleasantly into her champagne glass.

My eyes returned to the sea of lights beyond the window. "And over there is the tomb of Jinnah, the founder of Pakistan," said my friend, pointing to a cluster of distant lights.

I looked for the tomb of Jinnah.

Airports

INTERNATIONAL AIRPORTS DON'T really belong to nations. Rather, they are like independent sovereignties scattered around the world, interludes in time and space providing a sense of freedom and irresponsibility while we await flights to our next destinations. Within them, we are free of the mundane relationships and commitments that bind us to the world we left behind. We drink earlier than we normally drink, eat food we normally don't eat and read newspapers we normally wouldn't read.

These airports offer respite and security, something familiar, a routine we know. English is the common language and similar personnel tend our similar needs. Alter their pigmentation and facial features a bit and they would blend into any international airport of the world asking the same questions and performing the same services. After a sometimes harrowing taxi ride, a struggle with an unfamiliar culture or an anxious passage through immigration, we breathe sighs of relief as we bask once again in the comfortable familiarity of the transit lounge before taking off again.

Encounters in these airports are usually brief but occasionally intense with an instant comradery engendered by the ephemeral nature of the encounter. We are introduced to people for minutes—maybe hours— who then disappear forever from our lives. Because we know such encounters are fleeting, we sometimes reveal aspects of ourselves that we would otherwise not reveal and learn things about others we normally would not be told. Perhaps because we know we'll never meet again, we allow the intimacy to happen.

My flight departed Istanbul at 8 P.M. bound for a stopover at Tehran and then on to Karachi where I would visit a friend from graduate school days. The fasten-seatbelt light darkened and I settled into the three-hour flight.

For the first time, I noticed a small very elderly woman sitting beside me in a seat I thought was empty. She sustained a quiet frown beneath her unsleeping closed eyes but the other passengers were open-eyed with their hidden thoughts. Typical of international passengers in that part of the world, they included an African man in a brilliant dashiki, a trio of Japanese men in dark business suits, two Malay men in batik sarongs, an American teenager in blue jeans and red sweatshirt, two Arab women in black burkas with their white-robed spouses, three portly fez-capped Egyptians, and an array of Europeans and Middle Easterners in variations of Western garb. A few wanderers roamed the aisles to stretch legs and relieve anxieties while the flight attendants huddled together at the front enjoying a comradery denied them during the busy early minutes of takeoff. It was like a scene from a Technicolored film noir. I watched them and imagined the personal histories that brought them to this particular airplane.

Tired from a long day of sightseeing in Istanbul, I reclined my seat and slipped into a light slumber. After what seemed only minutes, I was awakened by an announcement instructing us to fasten our seatbelts in preparation for landing. I gazed out the window at Tehran's sea of lights below me, remembering that every city of the world is beautiful at night when viewed from above. But a closer look revealed large fires burning throughout the city. As I puzzled over the flames, the gigantic airplane made an amazingly smooth landing and taxied to the terminal. When we stopped, a voice over the PA told us disembarkation was delayed because of unspecified problems at the terminal. A chorus of groans greeted the announcement.

Beside me, the old woman opened her eyes and said resignedly, "So be it." She looked at me and added, "Do you think they got rid of him?"

"Who?" I asked.

"The Shah, of course. They've been trying to topple him for months. And for good reason. Not that his replacement will be much better. They rarely are."

I'd been traveling several weeks and was somewhat out of touch with international news. Headlines told me about the unrest in Iran but I hadn't read the stories too closely.

"Are you Iranian?" I asked.

"Do I look Iranian?" She paused. "I suppose I could be. Maybe I'll add that to my nationalities."

"You've moved about?"

"I've lived in four different countries but never left home. I think I'm Polish now but I haven't checked recently." Her English was heavily flavored with an accent I couldn't identify.

I laughed and said, "Sounds like a riddle."

"No riddle. The boundaries of Eastern Europe have been rather fluid the past few decades. They come and they go. I no longer take them seriously."

Another announcement crackled over the PA: "Please remain seated while security guards inspect the cabin." Apprehensive murmurs rippled among the passengers. The door opened and four angry-looking, bearded young men in military fatigues entered with automatic rifles. Two of them hurried to the back of the plane while the others remained at the front. One of them shouted in fractured English: "Remain seated. No one will be hurt."

Apprehensive silence replaced the cabin's murmurs. The soldiers walked slowly in the aisle carefully scrutinizing passengers.

"Boys playing with guns," the old woman beside me sighed. "I've seen all this so many times." The nearest soldier glared toward her and said something in Farsi. She replied loudly in English, "You don't frighten me. Take your gun away and you're a coward. I've known many like you."

They obviously had no understanding of one another's language. The soldier approached her angrily, but when he saw that she was an old woman, he retreated. One of the soldiers at the front shouted to the others and they all left the plane. Minutes later another PA announcement told us that all passengers must disembark. As we stood to retrieve overhead bags, the PA crackled to life again and announced that only passengers destined for Tehran could leave the plane.

"Make up your simple minds," grumbled the old woman. "Is anyone in charge here?"

Two of the armed men reappeared at the door and one of them shouted something in Farsi. Those who understood him filed from the plane. About half the passengers were now gone.

The old woman looked disgusted but said nothing. Yet again the PA sounded, this time announcing that the remaining passengers must exit the plane with their luggage. I helped the old woman retrieve her small black bag from the overhead bin and we exited into an uninviting concrete lounge harshly illuminated by fluorescent lights.

For the first time, I noticed the old woman's attire. She was dressed entirely in black, a loose-fitting smock-like dress, a heavy black sweater, black stockings and black brogues. She carried a black purse. Strands of white hair escaped from her black kerchief. Her complexion was ashen and her face deeply lined. She looked ancient and probably was. I followed her to seats against the far wall. Bent over and walking slowly in obvious discomfort, she carefully settled into a seat muttering quietly to herself, "It's so cruel when your jaded old mind wants to die but your aching body refuses to let go of life."

Sitting beside her, I introduced myself.

"Call me 'old woman'," she replied vaguely, look-ing straight ahead. "That's what I am to the world, an ugly old woman everyone looks through and never sees, a relic relegated to the trashcan of old age. If they saw what I've seen, maybe they wouldn't make the same stu-pid mistakes over and over. But they don't want to hear from me. Besides they can't be told. They must stumble through life to understand it—if understanding is possi-ble. Which it probably isn't."

Unsure of a proper response to this outpouring, I asked "What is your destination?" Two young soldiers moved throughout the room checking passports.

She ignored my question. I tried another tack. "Do you have children?"

She was silent for several moments and then said softly, "I had two children but they are gone." She paused. "I should never have brought children into this crazy, cruel world we have created."

I was running out of potential conversation top-ics when I noticed the three Egyptians talking together across the room. "I'll see if those men know what's going on. I'll be right back."

I approached the Egyptians and asked if they knew what was happening. One told me a Farsi-speaking passenger overheard the soldiers say the Shah was over-thrown and the city was in chaos. No one seemed to know much else. I returned to the old woman and related what I learned.

She appeared unconcerned as she studied the passen-gers scattered about the room. "Look at these people. On the streets they would not see me. No one looks at old people. They look through us as if we are invisible ghosts. They do not care that I was once a beautiful opera diva, that I was a resistance fighter against the Russians, that I am a celebrated poet. Do you believe me? Of course not. You think I'm a crazy old woman." She hesitated. "Maybe I am."

A gun-laden young soldier approached and said something I couldn't understand. I looked at him blankly and he shouted in English, "Passport!" I pulled my passport from my coat pocket, but the old woman made no move to retrieve hers.

"You foolish young man," she mumbled. She looked up at the soldier. "Do you understand what you're doing? No, you're too young to understand but let me tell you something. No cause is worth sacrificing your life. Your life is but a little blink on this tiny speck we call Earth. Enjoy it, don't waste it on a meaningless human cause. Put your gun away. Go home to your family wherever they are. You're sacrificing your life for someone else's words. Words, words, words. Words you don't understand. And it will all be repeated in twenty years or so with slightly different words. I've seen so many young men like you die for causes—empire, country, communism, Nazism, democracy. If life has taught me anything, it's taught me that nothing is worth dying for. Nothing. When you are dead, you are dead. There's nothing more. And there's no coming back."

The young soldier obviously understood nothing she said. He looked at her puzzled as he returned my passport. He quickly moved on without asking for hers.

"Where are you going?" I asked again as we watched the soldiers move about the room checking passports.

"My pious brother would say to Hell. But if he and his kind are going to Heaven, I'm glad I'm going to Hell. How can anyone believe in a god? Where's evidence of a god? If there's a god in charge of this mad world, he must be an evil god. Or a fool."

Once again the PA crackled to life: "All Karachi transit passengers must board the plane at gate twelve."

"Are you going to Karachi?" I asked the old woman.

She didn't answer immediately. "Yes, I suppose. But it really doesn't matter."

"I must use the restroom. I'll come back and accompany you to the plane."

The old woman said nothing.

When I emerged from the restroom minutes later, the old woman was gone from the seat where she was sitting. I wandered the room searching for her but I couldn't find her. My plane's final boarding was announced and I hurried to board.

A half-hour later I was in the air again. As I looked down at the fires burning throughout Tehran, I wondered if they were fires of celebration or fires of protest. Probably both. I remembered the old woman and wondered how her life had unfolded to create such cynicism in her final years. What had she lived through? What happened to her children? Was she really once a poet or an opera diva? A resistance fighter? I didn't know where she came from or where she was going.

Her seat beside me was empty.

*　　*　　*

I was collapsed in a tired chair at the Lima airport, recovering from a trip to the Amazon and Machu Picchu, and eager to depart Peru. It was not one of my easier trips. If anything, it was probably my most difficult one. All that could go wrong seemingly went wrong. My Lima hotel was raided by bandits, my Amazon cruise ship ran aground on a sandbar and my train from Machu Picchu derailed in the middle of the night. I suspected the trip might go awry when I watched attendants at the airport fuel the ancient airplane with buckets of gasoline filtered through an old T-shirt. The tires, smooth as peeled boiled eggs, were disconcerting too.

The international lounge was rather empty when I arrived but now fellow travelers were gathering, most on the older side, wrinkled and tired of travel—and some obviously tired of their traveling companions. Some visited Peru as a duty; tomorrow they would cross Peru off their lists and move on to the next country. Some were still digesting the spirituality of Machu Picchu, gushing platitudes and sentimental clichés. Others were appalled by Lima and couldn't leave soon enough. Two cities could not be more unlike: one, empty and ancient, soaring to the heavens and the other, crowded and contemporary, grounded in human debris.

Across the room, the young Dane I met on the Amazon surrendered his battered canvas bag at the ticket counter. He'd spent a week in an Indian village where he bit off the head of a snake during a hallucinogenic trance with an old shaman. Standing impatiently behind him was a chinless Chinese man who looked alarmingly like a weasel. And behind him stood the chubby Dutchman I met at Machu Picchu who told me his staid relatives back in Holland were *lived* by life rather than *living* it as he was. Sitting across the lounge, browsing through a ragged magazine, was the tall sixty-year-old Texas divorcée who sat beside me on the flight from Cusco. She was out to see the world on her own before her alimony ran out.

A burst of voices interrupted my musings. I glanced across the room and saw Maisie, the space-cadet on steroids who shared a bus seat with me on the way to the airport. An unmarried postal worker from Milwaukee, she was a nonstop-talking chain-smoker who discovered under hypnosis that she once lived at Machu Picchu during an earlier incarnation. She visited the site to see if it seemed familiar. It did, of course. Machu Picchu attracts lots of people like her desperately seeking something. Maisie was fiftyish and skinny, dressed in grubby shorts and an abbreviated halter. Her blood-red fingernails matched her frizzy hair which was only partially captured into a ponytail. She slouched like a limp pretzel and constantly shoved her heavy-framed glasses from the tip of her nose. Long dangly earrings sparkled from each ear and tired flip-flops adorned her equally tired feet. She plopped beside me and as if no time had lapsed continued talking where she'd left off when our bus arrived at the airport.

"My mother hates me, I can't stand her either. She always liked my brother better. Look at him now. A drunkard and a doper."

She pulled a stack of addressed postcards from her big pink purse. "I send a hundred cards each time I travel. I address them before I leave home. Instead of writing a journal, I write one sentence about what I'm doing on each card and send it off. No one knows everything I do, but everyone gets a sample." She scrawled on cards as she talked.

"That's one way to do it," I said.

She ignored me. "I've visited over a hundred countries. Peru is 102. Sometimes I forget the ones I've visited." She scratched at her left underarm. "That's why I keep a list. It's alphabetical."

She sucked on an unfiltered cigarette and returned it to the ashtray beside her. "I know I shouldn't smoke but I do anyway. My grandmother smoked a pack every day of her life and she lived to be ninety-five. Got hit by a bus. What's that tell you?"

I didn't attempt to squeeze in an answer.

"I take three vacations every year. Done it the past thirty years. Never had an accident or a problem. I know how to handle men if they bother me. Kick 'em in the balls." She continued writing on the stack of postcards. "I like hot places. I like to snorkel in the nude."

I shuddered at Maisie in the nude, snorkeling or otherwise.

"I'm an epileptic and shouldn't be snorkeling. But you gotta live life. If I die snorkeling I'd rather be food for the fish than polluting the earth in a coffin. I love to talk to people. I like to hear their stories."

I couldn't imagine her shutting up long enough to hear anyone's response let alone their stories.

"I like to play solitaire. But I cheat a lot. I hate to lose. I saw the king of Thailand once. Saw the queen of England too. I heard the Dalai Lama speak but I couldn't understand what he was saying. He giggled a lot." She took another long drag from her cigarette. "I think I saw Marlon Brando in Paris. Not sure. He was far away. But someone said it was him. I have nothing against gays."

She took another pull from her cigarette and blew smoke through her nose.

"Did I tell you I hate my brother? I'd like to kill the son-of-a-bitch. I probably shouldn't say that, but I would. I actually planned how I'd do it once."

She took a swig from an oversized paper coffee cup. She needed more caffeine like she needed a hole in her head.

"I love to dance and I go to discos wherever I travel. Last week some Koreans were making a film at an Amazon camp where they dressed Indians in grass skirts. I put on one of the skirts and danced with them. It was a hoot! They paid the Indians a dollar apiece. I got a dollar too." She laughed.

She quickly glanced around the room. "That man's too fat. Probably eats like a pig. He should go on a diet."

She was quiet for a moment, but only a moment, as she scribbled on a postcard. "I always stop by the same bar every night for a drink after work. Never more than one drink. Scotch. Johnny Walker Red. Then I go home and sit in my rocking chair looking out the window at the people on the street. Sometimes I start laughing, laughing at all the idiots out there. Have you noticed that most people in the world are idiots?"

She hurried on. "I don't have a cat or dog. Too much work. I hate dogs. Smelly and slobbery. Shit everywhere.

Once I had a goldfish but he died. I think it was a 'he.' Hard to tell with goldfish."

She paused and chewed on her thumbnail. "Broke my nail." She chewed it some more. "I never wanted kids. Too many people in the world. Never wanted to get married. Most men are jerks. Think they're so special because they got that little thing dangling between their legs."

A loud voice from the PA announced a flight to Santiago.

"That's me," said Maisie. She swept up her postcards and stuffed them into her purse, squashed out her cigarette and downed her remaining coffee. "Time for Chile." She flip-flopped across the lounge and disappeared through the departure gate.

Chicago's O'Hare is not one of my favorite airports. When I change flights there, I invariably walk for what seems like miles to make my connection. But that wasn't my problem this time. This time it was a blizzard. I was sitting in the departure lounge gazing out the window at winds hurling snow horizontally across the tarmac. I was eager to continue my trip, but my travel plans lacked urgency so I wasn't unduly upset that flights were indefinitely cancelled because of the blizzard.

I had finished my book, read the *New York Times*, eaten lunch, visited the john and now I was people-watching. Friends and families were keeping some of the delayed passengers company as they awaited their flights. This was the days before strict security rules barred everyone but passengers from the departure lounges. I noticed a well-dressed man sitting across the narrow aisle from me reading *The Wall Street Journal.* He was probably in his early forties and medium height with a full head of carefully coifed steel-gray hair. He wore a dark gray suit with a complementary paisley-patterned tie. His stylish black shoes were polished but not shiny. He was good-looking and knew it but not with conceit. He looked up at me, smiled and nodding toward the angry blizzard outside said, "It appears we're going to be here for a while."

"All indicators suggest that," I replied.

"What's your destination?" he asked, carefully folding his newspaper and placing it on the seat beside him.

"New York and then Madrid. And you?"

"London. And then home."

"And where's home?"

"Stratford."

"As in Stratford-on-Avon and Shakespeare?"

He smiled. "Yes, the one place in England beyond London that most Americans know."

"I'm embarrassed to admit I've never been there. Is it still a town where English people actually live ordinary lives or has it become a Disneyland tourist mecca?"

"Some of both. I don't actually live in Stratford. My family's estate is a few miles away in the country."

For the first time, I noticed that his speech was not quite American but not entirely English either.

"So your family has lived there for some time?"

"Since the 1500s and maybe longer according to an ancient aunt who enjoys researching that sort of thing."

"And are you related to Shakespeare?" I asked somewhat facetiously.

He laughed. "Believe it or not, Aunt Margaret claims we are. Through the Hart side of my family that supposedly has connections to Shakespeare's mother. But I take it all with a healthy grain of salt." He then asked me, "What part of the States are you from?"

"I've lived in San Francisco many years. Do you know the States?"

"Probably better than most Englishmen. I went to school at Yale and lived on the East Coast several years when I was younger. I came back a few years ago."

"That explains some of the American accent I hear."

He smiled. "My family tells me I sound like an American."

"Probably with chagrin."

"Not really. We have American kin connections. And my wife was American."

"She's English now?"

"No." His mood suddenly changed. "I'm afraid she's dead now."

"I'm so sorry."

After an awkward silence, he said, "I'm returning to England for her funeral. She was murdered three days ago."

"How horrible. What a terrible shock for you. What happened?" A long silence followed. "I'm sorry. If you don't want to talk about it, I understand."

"I don't mind. It happened at our home. She was stabbed in the chest repeatedly and her throat was slit."

"Oh my god!" I was genuinely shocked. "I . . . I don't know what to say."

"I understand. I shouldn't have told you. I'm sorry, but I feel a need to talk about it."

"When did you last see her?"

"I haven't seen her in a year or so. We lived apart."

"Do you have children?"

He paused. "Yes . . . two. They died young." He paused again. "To be honest with you, I always thought she killed them."

"What on earth makes you believe that?"

"She never wanted children. Both deaths were attributed to SIDS. I accepted the first death without question. But when our second child died, I became convinced that my wife suffocated her. I never pursued an investigation. I had no evidence. But in my heart I still believe she killed those babies."

"It must be awful to live with that belief."

"That's the chief reason I chose to stay here in the States. We haven't lived together for some time."

"Will you stay in England or do you plan to return to the States?"

"I'll probably come back someday, but it'll be a while before I can. Mother died recently and the family estate has passed to me. I want to sell it and rid myself of all that past. I've no desire to live in that ancient house, but some family members oppose its sale. But it's my decision and I intend to sell. It's a valuable property and I should have no trouble selling it. I don't need the money. I have more money than I can ever spend. But I want to sever my ties with England. They are not happy ties." He looked at his watch and asked me, "What time do you have? I don't think my watch is correct."

I glanced at my watch and said, "One o'clock."

"I must make a telephone call," he said, standing up. "Thank you for talking with me. I'm afraid it wasn't a pleasant conversation."

"I hope all turns out as well as possible for you."

"Thank you." He walked from the lounge and disappeared in the crowd of travelers.

As I digested the disturbing story, I decided my body needed some movement. I walked to the window and watched the blizzard. Then I went to a nearby newsstand where the publications offered nothing appealing. I noticed a shoeshine stand on the other side of the lounge. A glance at my shoes told me they could use some help. I seldom patronize shoeshine stands, but I had time to kill and it seemed a good way to pass some minutes. An old Italian-looking man with a droopy moustache saw me approaching and invited me to an empty chair. I complied.

"Where you headed for?" he asked as I hiked up my trousers.

"New York," I said, "but it may be awhile before I get there."

"The storm's supposed to blow itself out this afternoon. Flights will probably start again this evening. I saw you talking to Will. Who's he today?"

"Will? Who's Will?"

"That guy you were talking to. I call him Will. Sometimes he tells people he's related to William Shakespeare."

"You know him?"

"Nah. Not really." He applied polish to my shoes. "He comes in here every now and then and talks to passengers. He tells some big whoppers. Once he claimed he was President Roosevelt's grandson. Another time he said he was Marilyn Monroe's old boyfriend before she became famous. Usually someone dies or gets killed in his stories. He's a real nut case, but he's harmless."

"Who is he really?"

"Beats me. Probably one of the crazies from Chicago." He began buffing my shoes. "A lot of weirdos live there. I first noticed him about three years ago, maybe two. Some of my customers tell me the stories he tells 'em. He told one guy that his father invented the atomic bomb but didn't get credit for it." He chuckled to himself. "What'd he tell you?"

Pacific Passage

I NEEDED A LONG uninterrupted block of writing time for a book I was trying to finish. One day while considering possibilities, a popular song from the 1940s called "Slow Boat to China" kept popping into my thoughts. "Why not?" I decided. A slow boat to China would provide the time I needed for writing. Or more specifically a slow freighter to Hong Kong—China was still pretty much off-limits to Americans back in those days. My travel agent booked me on a freighter departing Oakland destined for Hong Kong with stops in Japan, Korea, Okinawa and Taiwan. From Hong Kong I would fly to the Philippines and visit a fellow anthropologist at her field site in northeastern Luzon before returning to San Francisco.

I chose the freighter because of its Spartan accommodations and limited distractions. It provided a cabin and meals but not much else. No twenty-four hour bars, buffets and entertainment as on the luxury liners that were becoming increasingly available to middle class

Americans in the early 1980s. The freighter accepted only twelve passengers and offered no diversions except old movies shown nightly in the passenger lounge. Lots of time for writing.

Three friends drove me to the Port of Oakland where we located the terminal and boarded a ship the size of a football field, its deck stacked with containers. A smiling Filipino crewman welcomed us aboard and directed us to my cabin where we opened a bottle of champagne and talked the sort of talk people talk when filling time before a departure. After the champagne, we went on deck and watched giant cranes load the final containers onto the ship. Finally at about ten P.M., visitors were told to disembark and my friends left. I returned to my cabin and unpacked. We wouldn't depart for at least another hour but I remained dressed so I could go on deck when the ship passed under the Golden Gate Bridge. I sprawled out on the bed, dozing fitfully before falling into a deep slumber. When I awakened, the ship was moving. I hurried outside and watched the Golden Gate Bridge disappear into the fog.

The next morning, I took a quick shower, dressed and waited for the bell that according to the notice on my wall would announce breakfast. It rang and I followed signs down the hallway to the dining room where I located my assigned table. Each of the five tables in the room seated four people and displayed numbered placards. As I was considering the blandness of the room and imagining what a talented decorator would do to it, an elderly couple appeared. Both were seriously spherical and seemed competing to see who could become the roundest. The man was winning. They smiled wide good mornings and located their table at the opposite side of the room. As they settled into their chairs—no small feat—a young African-American woman appeared from the kitchen with a pot of coffee.

She greeted me and smilingly announced that breakfast would be served when the other passengers arrived. Seemingly on cue, the others all arrived. A tall, trim elderly woman spotted the number on my table and approached. Her hair was bluish and her face probably once pretty. Now it was matronly and pleasant.

"I'm afraid you're stuck with me for the voyage," she laughed. "I'm told that table assignments can't be altered, barring shipwreck and civil strife. My name is Dorothy Benton." She extended her hand. I stood, took her hand and introduced myself. She sat in the opposite chair as the waitress approached with coffee.

Two petite elderly women coifed in blond pageboy wigs and dressed identically in flowing shades of lavender entered the room and offered small smiles as they joined the round couple. A middle-aged man and woman chose the table opposite me, offering no smiles or greetings to anyone. They perused the menu studiously while the woman lighted a small bejeweled pipe. People smoked everywhere back in those days, but not too many women smoked pipes, bejeweled or otherwise. The waitress moved about the room offering tea or coffee as the passengers exchanged furtive glances.

Suddenly an irritating male voice sounded from the hallway: "You're always late. You knew the bell would ring at eight, but you fussed as usual until the last minute. I don't know how I've tolerated you all these years."

A frail pencil-thin angry-looking man entered the room with an attractive slim woman at his side. They were probably in their early seventies.

"What's our table number? Did you remember to check it? Probably not."

"I remembered," she said. "It's number four."

My tablemate and I exchanged glances. Our table was number four. The man approached aggressively and announced without introduction, "We've been assigned to this table. But it looks like there are empty tables and I hope we can take one of them. We prefer to eat alone." I shared his hope for separate tables and the expression on Dorothy's face suggested her concurrence.

As they settled into their chairs, Dorothy and I introduced ourselves. The man reluctantly told us that he was Horace Hayes and his wife was Pearl. He studied his menu unhappily as his wife acknowledged us with a smile.

A uniformed man entered the room, identified himself as the purser and asked us to join him in the passenger lounge following breakfast where he would tell us more about our voyage. He seated himself as three other officers entered and joined him at the tables reserved for them away from us passengers.

"That woman is smoking a pipe!" muttered Horace Hayes under his breath. "That is disgusting." He shivered slightly.

"It's unusual," said his wife.

"Of course, you would defend her," said Hayes.

"I simply said it's unusual."

Hayes glared at her and returned to the menu. I noticed an Agatha Christie novel beside Pearl Hayes' plate. "Are you a Christie fan?" I asked, attempting conversation.

Before she could answer, her husband said, "That's the sort of trash she reads."

"She and some of the rest of us," said Dorothy, icily.

He stared at her coldly and slapped his menu to the table. "Why do they give us a menu if there are no choices?"

"Perhaps to let us know what to expect," suggested Dorothy.

Hayes looked at her unpleasantly and said, "We're not interested in conversing during meals."

Dorothy glanced at me, rolled her eyes and muttered, "Whatever." She sipped her coffee.

After breakfast, I accompanied Dorothy to the passenger lounge where the purser greeted us. When everyone was seated, the ship's captain appeared, a tall gray-haired man probably in his early fifties. He introduced himself, recited some scripted words of welcome, said the purser would explain the ship's rules and then departed. The purser asked us to introduce ourselves.

Dorothy and I began the introductions followed by Horace and Pearl Hayes. The identically dressed women, who by now I realized were twins, were next. One said rather primly, "I'm Orpha Olson, and ..." She glanced at the woman beside her who said, "and I am Olive Olson." Olive continued, "We are twins." Orpha added, "And we are from Oakley, Oklahoma." Olive concluded, "Think of us as the five O's—Olive and Orpha Olson from Oakley, Oklahoma." I suspected this was one of their stock lines. We all chuckled courteously—except Horace Hayes. The woman of the rotund couple announced that they were Julie-Josephine and Norman Redroad from Albany, South Carolina. The pipe-smoking woman and her husband turned out to be Liz and Ed Rainer from Denver. As I listened to the introductions, I realized that at forty, I was by far the youngest in the group. The Rainers were probably in their mid-fifties; the others in their seventies, the twins perhaps older.

The purser explained the ship's rules, most of which were posted in our cabins. He told us what areas of the ship we were allowed to visit, mostly the few portions of the deck not stacked with containers where we could walk, exercise and sunbathe. We were, however, advised to stay indoors if the seas were rough. Every evening at seven o'clock, movies would be shown in the passengers' lounge. We learned that last minute cancellations resulted in two passengers short of the usual twelve. When he completed his presentation, he entertained questions.

Horace Hayes immediately announced, "My wife and I are not accustomed to eating with strangers. We request a table for ourselves."

"I'm sorry, sir, but the assigned seating arrangements will prevail throughout the voyage."

"But there are empty tables. Why can't we have one of them?"

"There is only one half-empty table, sir. If you are moved, it would be to that table and you would be sharing it with another couple." The Rainers looked none too happy about that possibility.

"This is outrageous," fumed Hayes. "Had we known this, we would have reconsidered this trip."

"You were informed that passengers must abide by the ship's rules, sir. We sent you a rather extensive packet of information. I hope you read it."

"Of course, I read it." Hayes glared at the purser. "If you're finished, we are returning to our cabin."

The purser said we could leave if there were no other questions. Hayes stomped out with his wife meekly following, offering an apologetic smile to the room.

Dorothy leaned toward me and whispered, "What an ass."

The purser left and we dispersed to our various pursuits. Mine was back to my cabin where I slipped into writing until the lunchtime bell informed me it was eating-time again.

When I arrived at the dining room, Pearl Hayes was sitting at the table with Dorothy. They acknowledged my arrival as I sat between them.

"Horace will not be joining us," explained Pearl. "His stomach is bothering him and he thought it best to remain in the cabin. The kitchen has kindly prepared him a lunch."

"I'm sorry to hear he's not well," I said disingenuously, relieved that the unpleasant old man was absent and wondering if I could tolerate him the entire voyage.

Several mornings later I was in my cabin reluctantly preparing to write. I wasn't in the mood and the muses weren't speaking. I poked at my keyboard, lay on my bed and paced the floor until I decided a stroll on the deck might awaken the muses. It was a gray foggy day punctuated by the ship's moaning foghorns. A small cluster of seagulls perched atop a container suspiciously eyed me as if wondering what I was doing outside when I could be in my warm cabin. Apparently finding morsels in the water stirred by the ship's passing, the gulls had followed us from Oakland and were the only visible inhabitants of the lonely watery world encircling us. I had no idea where five days from Oakland had taken us, but I did know it would take twelve days to reach Yokohama, our first stop in Asia. The persistent moaning of the foghorns and the chill of the fog cut my stroll short and I returned to my cabin. I sat at my typewriter, still uninspired. I decided to check out the passenger lounge.

Dressed in cascading canary yellow muumuus and white scarves, the Olson twins sat at a table immersed in a game of Scrabble. Their wardrobes were always a circus of colors and each day presented a new combination in their ongoing fashion show. Dorothy and Pearl occupied a couch, each with a cup of coffee on the low table before them, enjoying a friendly conversation without the unpleasant cloud of Horace.

"Did you see Horace?" Pearl asked me. "He said he might take a walk on the deck."

I told her I hadn't seen him.

"He must have changed his mind. I never know what his mood will be."

"Sounds like my husband," said Dorothy.

"He's unpredictable?" asked Pearl.

"I haven't seen him in years. We divorced long ago. One of the best things that ever happened to me. The marriage was awful."

"Sometimes they are," said Pearl, following a brief silence.

"Do you have children?" I asked Pearl.

After a pause, she said, "No. I wanted children so badly, but Horace doesn't like children. He wouldn't even consider it." Following another pause, she added, "I became pregnant and he insisted I have an abortion."

I was hearing more than I wanted to know.

"He made you have an abortion?" asked Dorothy, incredulously. "That's horrible."

"Yes. It went badly and I ended up having a hysterectomy. And then there was no possibility of children. But maybe it was for the best. It wouldn't have been easy raising a child with Horace."

I noticed a Sherlock Holmes novel beside Pearl's coffee cup and latched onto it as a conversation-changer. "You seem to like British detective fiction," I said, nodding toward the novel.

"My escapist fare," she laughed. "I've read them all, most of them several times. Especially Agatha Christie. She creates an orderly comfortable world. Murders upset it, but one of her detectives comes along and solves the crime and order is restored. Everything ends happily except for those who don't deserve a happy ending. If only life were really that way."

"Do you read other writers?" I asked.

"Mostly British ones. I could commit the perfect crime if I lived in England but I'm not sure the formula would work in America." She laughed.

"I'll keep a cautious eye on you," I said.

The Redroads entered the lounge. Julie-Josephine carried a large bag overflowing with knitting needles and a pale blue unidentifiable wooly work-in-progress. Norman clutched a cluster of magazines. They smiled greetings and settled onto the couch opposite us. The couch groaned sadly. More company than I wanted was accumulating so I bid the lounge farewell and returned to my cabin hoping for a more productive encounter with my typewriter.

I was late in joining Dorothy and the Hayes for lunch. "I hope you haven't been waiting for me," I said.

"No," said Hayes. "They are late with lunch. As usual."

"It's only a few minutes after twelve," observed Pearl.

Hayes looked at her distastefully.

"Already I miss my little dog Casper," said Dorothy, obviously trying to change the subject.

"Oh, you have a dog," said Pearl. "I love dogs. If Horace weren't allergic to them we would have one."

"We certainly would not," snapped Hayes. "Smelly, dirty, noisy beasts. I would never have one in the house. Cats too. They belong outside, far away from me."

Pearl ignored him. "I always had a dog when I was a child. After all these years, I still miss having one around."

"I can't imagine living without a dog," said Dorothy.

"And I can't imagine living *with* one," said Hayes. He shuddered visibly.

The waitress arrived and Hayes conspicuously looked at his watch and then at the clock on the wall. Lunch was five minutes late.

I never learned much about the Rainers from Denver. They were polite, but distant and obviously not interested in interacting with the rest of us. Because of the last minute cancellations, they enjoyed the luxury of a table by themselves. Horace Hayes envied their empty chairs, but the purser was adamant in not altering seating, apparently thinking it might trigger other requests for changes and probably also to spite Horace Hayes. Like the rest of us, he obviously didn't like the old man. I sometimes met the Rainers on deck during my strolls; they always smiled, said hello and moved on. Rumors circulated that Ed Rainer was recovering from heart surgery and the voyage was his reward for surviving it. Each evening after dinner, Liz pulled out her jewel-encrusted pipe and lit-up. I never saw it close enough to know if they were real jewels or fakes, as if I could tell the difference. It didn't seem the healthiest accompaniment to her husband's recent surgery, but apparently that wasn't an issue for them. They never appeared in the lounge for the evening movies. As far as I knew, except for their strolls on the deck and their meals in the dining room, they spent all their time in their cabin. Only once they joined a sightseeing excursion when we reached Asia. And that's about all I learned of them.

On the other hand, I came to know more than I really cared to know about the chubby Redroads of South Carolina. Norman was round as a beach ball, his head bald and his face puffed and florid. Julie-Josephine shared his shape with the addition of oversized breasts and carefully coiffed white curls. They had many cruises under their substantial belts, so many they couldn't remember them all. I initially attributed their wanderlust to a curiosity about the world until I learned that in those days before the instant interconnectedness of the planet, their cruises made them unavailable to their three children who were always in need of a bailout of one sort or another. Julie-Josephine was the daughter of a Southern Baptist minister and Norman was the retired president of their local bank with a drinking problem they both tried to conceal. I never saw him drinking, but neither was I ever in his presence when he didn't smell of alcohol. One evening when he fell in the lounge, Julie-Josephine immediately said he suffered from vertigo. If it was vertigo, it was alcohol-induced vertigo fed by the stash of booze he apparently kept in his cabin. Once during a rare sunny day on the deck, I encountered Julie-Josephine sunbathing in shorts and halter with Norman in spandex briefs. Mr. and Mrs. Moby Dick flashed unkindly through my mind as I passed them, averting my eyes from their expansive white flesh.

I became fairly well acquainted with Pearl, but I saw little of her husband even though we were assigned the same dining table. He never appeared at breakfast and was frequently absent for other meals, often claiming illness and sometimes conning the staff into serving him in his cabin. He brought a variety of prepared foods, anticipating that he wouldn't care for that served aboard ship. It was always a relief to be spared his company. On the other hand, I enjoyed the company of kind-hearted Pearl. During our later sightseeing daytrips away from the ship when we reached Asia, she always carried bread or crackers in her purse to feed birds. She routinely gave coins to the beggars who approached us and usually managed to find something to feed the mangy stray dogs we sometimes encountered.

Pearl and Dorothy formed a close shipboard friendship and spent much time together when Horace wasn't around. Dorothy shared with me what she learned about Hayes, frequently more than I cared to know. Some evenings Pearl joined us in the lounge to watch movies. I wondered how she managed to escape her husband until Dorothy told me that she sometimes mixed a sleeping pill into his evening medications so she could slip away while he slept.

Dorothy, of course, disliked Hayes and as she learned more about him, her dislike intensified. She always called him "Horrible Horace" when we were alone. According to her, he never allowed Pearl to pursue a job even though she was trained as a nurse. She was an only child and inherited a modest legacy from her parents that Hayes insisted on managing and eventually transferred to his name. He gave Pearl an allowance and she provided receipts for all her expenditures. He dictated the clothes she wore and even decided the tint of her hair. The more I learned about the man, the more repulsive he became.

One evening when Hayes was absent, Pearl, Dorothy and I lingered over coffee in the lounge. We were alone except for the Olsons who were outfitted in their usual cornucopia of colors on the opposite side of the room where they played Scrabble.

"Do you and Horace travel frequently?" asked Dorothy.

"Oh no. Horace doesn't like to leave home. He had gall bladder surgery last spring and his doctor recommended complete rest. He's such a fussbudget. I knew he would never rest at home so I suggested we take a cruise where there'd be no distractions. He was opposed to it, of course—mostly because I suggested it. But when his doctor thought it a good idea, he became enthusiastic and planned the cruise."

"And is he enjoying it?"

Pearl smiled resignedly. "Of course not. Horace never enjoys anything. Surely you've noticed that." She paused. "And he usually makes sure I don't either. You wouldn't believe what he's subjected me to over the years."

"I've seen glimpses of it," muttered Dorothy, rolling her eyes at me.

Pearl continued. "When he was young, he drank a good deal. In fact, he drank heavily until recently, until he had his surgery." There was a long pause. "He was so abusive, verbally, not physically. I think I could have dealt with physical abuse easier than some of the awful things he said. It was terrible."

"Why on earth didn't you leave him?" asked Dorothy.

Pearl was quiet for several moments. "I was afraid of him. It's probably difficult for you to believe, but he was a big strong man back then. I had nowhere to go. I had no money. No job. No family. No friends. What could I do?"

"It's not too late," said Dorothy.

"But what does it matter now? I'm an old woman. It's all in the past."

"You may be an old woman, but you're not dead. There's more life for you to live," said Dorothy.

"You don't understand. I don't have the will to leave him." She paused and then said slowly, "But each morning when I awaken, I check to see if he's still breathing. He always is and I'm always disappointed."

The days rolled by and life at sea fell into a predictable routine bordering on boredom. The ship provided no entertainment beyond the evening movies in the lounge. One day the purser gave us a tour of the inner workings of the vessel, the extent of our venture beyond our assigned spaces. My days were filled with nonevents—eating, writing, eating, writing, napping, eating, writing and then sleeping. Meals became special occasions breaking the lassitude of the days. At times I felt like Pavlov's dog as I eagerly responded to the bell announcing a meal. Each day I spent time on deck for exercise and a break from my cabin but the weather was often depressingly gray and chilly. I never saw another ship or any trace of land. Occasionally I encountered other passengers on deck, but since we were all seeking privacy, conversation was limited to pleasantries, except old man Hayes who never acknowledged anyone's presence—and certainly was never pleasant. Turbulent seas tossed the ship some days but surprisingly no one became seasick as we were heaved onward toward Asia.

The Hayes and I were the only neophytes among the passengers, the others had all taken numerous freighter voyages. When planning the cruise, I thought my fellow passengers would be an interesting lot, seasoned vagabonds seeking more adventuresome venues than the standard tours. I was wrong. Although they certainly considered themselves world travelers—indeed some had visited all the continents—their knowledge of foreign places was mostly acquired from the deck of a freighter, their protected bit of Americana. When in port, they occasionally joined day excursions into the city, although the Olson twins thought most cities were too dirty and rarely left the ship except to visit nearby souvenir shops. The few officers and crewmen I met were only slightly worldlier. I expected more from men who'd spent their lives moving from one foreign port to another but beyond the stereotypes of most Americans, they knew little about the Asian cultures they routinely visited. Considering the nature of their voyages to Asia however, it wasn't surprising. They piloted the ship across the Pacific, stopping briefly in each port where the container-technology rapidly dispersed and collected cargo. Sometimes the ship was in port only a few hours before it moved on to the next port and then back to the States. Most of the crew rarely went ashore except to occasionally visit a nearby seaman's club.

*   *   *

One evening I was sitting in the lounge waiting for "Casablanca" to begin. I'd seen the film several times but was ready to give it another try. It was one of the rare occasions when Horace attended. Normally I would've found an excuse to leave, but I assumed he would watch the film quietly and spare us his acerbic tongue. Everyone was there except the Olsons.

"I love this movie," announced Julie-Josephine, her knitting needles clicking away at something yellow and fuzzy. "I've seen it so many times but I always cry at the end."

"I must admit that I do too," laughed Dorothy. "Each time I see it, I think I'll be bored but I never am."

Horace looked at them distastefully. As he was about to speak, the Olsons entered the lounge dressed in pink pantsuits with flowing scarlet scarves and white heels. "Good evening everyone," said Orpha leading Olive to the remaining empty chairs.

Horace glared at them and said, "Do you have any idea how silly you two look in those ridiculous outfits you wear? Don't you ever wear clothes appropriate to your age? You're pathetic."

"Oh no, Horace!" cried Pearl.

The twins looked stunned.

"But they always look so lovely," said Julie-Josephine, looking up perplexed from her knitting. "Everything is cheerier when they enter the room."

Norman added, "You're out of line Hayes." It was the first time I'd heard him utter a complete sentence.

Dorothy glared at Hayes silently and then exploded. "You odious old toad! You're the pathetic one. The Olsons always brighten the day. You sour everything."

Horace stood and stuttered apoplectically at Dorothy, "I will not put up with you." He looked around the room. "None of you. Come Pearl." He stomped from the room.

Pearl turned to the Olsons and said, "I'm so sorry. As always, you look lovely. Horace can be so cruel." She paused momentarily, turned and left the room.

The following afternoon I took a break from writing and visited the deck. The Olsons were seated in deck chairs resplendent in purple jump suits, matching brimmed hats and lavender scarves. Hayes' critique of their wardrobes hadn't dampened their style. I joined them in the remaining chair and asked them as a conversation starter: "Do the two of you live in the same town?"

"Oh yes. In the same house," replied Orpha as if any other arrangement were unthinkable. "The house where we were born."

"We were only three pounds each at birth," added Olive. "And now look at us." She giggled.

"Remarkable," I offered, unable to think of anything more appropriate. "I hope you weren't upset by Hayes last night. He was an ass, as usual. We all enjoy your colorful outfits and look forward to your entrance each day."

"Mr. Hayes is a dreadful man," said Orpha.

"Now Orpha . . ." cautioned her sister.

"I will not be shushed," said Orpha firmly. "He's an awful man. I feel so sorry for poor Pearl having to live with him. Such men make us thankful that we chose to never marry. I don't know why she stays with him. Someone should shove him overboard."

"Oh Orpha!"

"Come now, Olive. I don't mean *really* shove him overboard. You know what I mean. He's a malicious old man and Pearl shouldn't have to put up with him."

"It seems so many couples grow to dislike one another," mused Olive. "Have you noticed? It starts out so good and then it sours." She paused. "I suppose it helps when children come along."

"Children only make it worse," said Orpha emphatically. "Then you have to pretend you like them."

Olive laughed, "We were probably wise to remain old maids."

"You mean 'independent women'," Orpha corrected her sister severely.

Several days after talking to the Olsons, I arrived early for breakfast, anticipating a solitary cup of coffee before the others appeared. Such was not to be. No sooner was I served than Dorothy arrived. She uttered a quiet hello and sat across from me and resumed reading a magazine, apparently also seeking some coffee and quiet time. Moments later, a very distraught Pearl Hayes appeared.

"I can't find Horace anywhere," she exclaimed when she saw us. "Have you seen him?"

"I haven't seen him," I said. "I came here directly from my cabin."

"Same here," said Dorothy. "Have you looked in the lounge? Maybe he's on the deck."

"I checked both places and he's not there."

"When did you last see him?" I asked.

"Last night. He was reading when I went to bed. I took a sleeping pill and didn't wake up until about an hour ago. He was gone. Where could he be?" She was becoming more distraught.

"He couldn't have gone far," said Dorothy. "Have a cup of coffee? I'm sure he'll show up."

"Something has happened. I know. This isn't like him."

"Maybe he's visiting some of the other passengers," I suggested.

She looked at me incredulously and said, "He would never do that." I silently agreed that it seemed unlikely.

The Olsons entered, dazzling in orange floral-patterned muumuus. They responded negatively when Pearl asked if they'd seen Hayes—as did the Redroads who were directly behind them.

"This is so unlike him," said Pearl.

"Let's talk to the purser," suggested Dorothy, standing. "I'm sure there's a simple explanation."

"I'll come with you," I volunteered.

We met the Rainers in the hallway and they too had not seen Hayes. We encountered the purser leaving his office and Pearl told him Horace was missing. He suggested we return to the dining room while he checked the likely places where Horace might be. Reluctantly, Pearl accompanied Dorothy and me back to the dining room where breakfast was being served. Pearl fidgeted with her food as Dorothy and I made futile attempts to engage her in conversation. None of the crew arrived for breakfast and I assumed they were helping the purser track down Hayes. As we finished our final cup of coffee, the captain and the purser appeared.

"Have you found him?" Pearl anxiously asked as soon as she saw them.

"Not yet, but we're still looking," replied the captain. "When did you last see him?"

Pearl repeated the story she told us earlier. Horace was reading in an easy chair when she went to bed. She's a light sleeper and consequently took her usual sleeping pill when she retired and didn't awaken until morning. Horace was gone, but the reading lamp was still on and his book was on the desk. He'd not changed into his pajamas and his jacket was missing.

The captain asked the other passengers if they'd seen Horace during the night. None had. The Rainers had walked on deck before retiring at about ten o'clock and hadn't seen anyone. The others had remained in their cabins until morning after watching the film in the lounge. The captain assured Pearl that her husband would be found.

But he was not found. The ship's entire crew joined the search and went over the vessel with a fine-toothed comb. Every nook and cranny and crevice was probed, but no trace of Horace Hayes turned up. Everyone was puzzled at his disappearance but to say we were grieved would be untrue. He was an extremely unpleasant old man and had no friends among us. Only Pearl was upset.

That evening after dinner, I took my usual stroll on deck before settling into my cabin. It was a windless night with a full moon occasionally obscured by scudding clouds. After pacing the portion of the deck allotted passengers, I settled into a deckchair to watch the parade of clouds crossing the moon, remembering the childhood game of identifying familiar shapes in cloud formations. The sound of a closing door interrupted my reverie. Pearl Hayes emerged from the shadows. She didn't see me. She was carrying two shopping bags and walked determinedly to the rail of the ship where she tossed both bags overboard. She remained at the rail several minutes watching the same cloud activity I was watching. She turned and started when she saw me.

"I'm sorry," she said. "I thought I was alone."

"Only me," I said. "The moon is beautiful, isn't it?"

"Yes, yes it is," she replied absently and then added quickly, "You probably wonder what I threw overboard."

Indeed I did, but I said nothing.

"Some clothes," she volunteered. "Some clothes Horace chose for me. I hated them. He's gone now and I'll never have to wear them again. I've packed all his belongings into his suitcases and I'll give them to the purser in the morning. I want nothing of his." She turned abruptly and reentered the ship.

I continued watching the restless clouds, thinking that Pearl seemed rather certain her husband would not be found.

The following day the captain and purser interviewed each passenger individually regarding Hayes' final hours, but we could offer little to what was already known. We'd all seen him at lunch and dinner the day before his disappearance but remembered nothing unusual that would explain his absence. Eventually, the captain concluded that Hayes must have fallen overboard, although how that happened was unclear. A high railing surrounded the deck area allotted to passengers. The sea was not particularly turbulent on the night he disappeared so it seemed unlikely a wave swept him from the deck as Olive Olson proposed. When the captain suggested he'd committed suicide, Pearl was appalled at the suggestion. He'd left no note and he certainly didn't seem the suicidal type. The captain announced that an official investigation into the affair would be conducted when we reached Yokohama where we would probably be questioned further.

We were two days from Yokohama. When we reached the Japanese port, the captain summoned us to the lounge and announced that all passengers would be interviewed about Hayes' disappearance by the shipping line's Yokohama representatives. Pearl was questioned first while the rest of us waited in the lounge. About fifteen minutes later, I was summoned. A pleasant middle-aged man sat behind a desk and his younger colleague occupied an easy chair. I was unable to supply them with any new information. After all of us were interviewed, we were told that we'd be informed of their conclusion when it was determined. The following day I joined some of the other passengers for a quick tour of Yokohama and then we were at sea once again.

After leaving Yokohama, the voyage became much more scenic as we made our way through the Inland Sea of Japan. Japan is a beautiful collection of islands, some however hideously scarred by gashes of industrialization. Dotted with ferries, freighters and fishing boats, the Inland Sea was populated by many little islands muffled in soft gray mists. Occasionally one emerged, loomed before us and then retreated back into grayness.

Busan was next. Fog delayed our entrance into the bay but once docked, we left the ship for a few hours in the city. Korea lacked the compulsive cleanliness of Japan, but in many ways its sights, sounds and smells seemed much more Asian. Dorothy and I were the only ones who opted for the sightseeing trip at Okinawa. The others thought it would be a repeat of Japan but it wasn't and I enjoyed its differences—and I also enjoyed the time away from the other passengers. Our brief glimpse of Taiwan was afforded through the southern port of Kaohsiung. Vistas of China appeared as we moved on toward Hong Kong. From the sea, China was a land with lots of little islands scattered off its coast. In the early morning we passed several junks, their orange batwing sails reminiscent of a more ancient China. And finally we reached the bustling Hong Kong harbor—and the end of my voyage.

After the ship berthed, the captain called us into the passenger lounge where he informed us the official investigation into Horace Hayes' disappearance concluded that he had accidently fallen overboard or committed suicide. Neither seemed likely to me but I could offer no better explanation. Pearl listened to the announcement emotionless. The rest of us remained silent entertaining private speculations.

*   *   *

Dorothy and I were sitting with Pearl at the Hong Kong airport awaiting the flights that would separate us for our continuing journeys—mine to Manila, Dorothy to Calcutta and Pearl back to San Francisco. When Pearl's flight was announced, she stood and said, "It's time to say good-bye."

Dorothy embraced her warmly and said, "I have your address and phone number. We'll stay in touch." Both women were moist-eyed, having become close friends during the voyage. Dorothy added, "Remember, you're entering a new chapter of your life and I know it'll be a good one. And you've found a new friend. I'll always be here for you. And don't forget we're seeing Paris in the fall."

"Indeed we are, dear Dorothy." They embraced again.

Pearl turned to me and we shook hands. "I wish you well," I said. She returned my wishes and walked toward her gate, merging into the crowd and disappearing through the departure door.

"I wonder if we'll ever know what happened to Horace," I mused as we watched Pearl depart. "What an awful man. I wouldn't blame her if she shoved him overboard."

Dorothy smiled at me as the PA announced the boarding of her flight. "Pearl didn't shove him overboard." She picked up her small carry-on. "Take my word for it. *She* didn't shove him overboard." She sauntered toward her gate, gave me an over-the-shoulder wave and added, "Stay in touch."

Puccini in Burma

THE OLD RANGOON airport is without doubt the most challenging airport I encountered in my many travels. Back in those days before Burma became Myanmar, visitors were allowed only one week in the country. Chaotic was the only word for the confusion in the cavernous room where arriving visitors were herded. No signs told them anything about the procedure. Everyone was eager to pass through immigration so they could cram as much sightseeing as possible into their limited stay. They shoved, pushed and shouted their ways to the counter where they received a handful of barely legible and almost unintelligible mimeographed forms to fill out. They completed them as quickly as possible, shoved their way back to the counter where stony-faced Burmese bureaucrats enjoyed their place of power in the spotlight. It was night and the tropical heat was oppressive.

A few of us, deciding to wait until the mob thinned, found spaces on the worn benches scattered around the room illuminated by flickering fluorescent fixtures probably from the Russian era of interest in the country. An exasperated couple who looked American eased from the mob and surveyed the room for a bench. They headed toward me. The woman would stand out in any crowd, but she especially stood out in this ill-behaved motley melee of tourists in their wrinkled travel garb. She was probably in her mid-forties, tall and large—not over-weight, a big woman—with reddish blond hair piled atop her head. Her striking hazel eyes were almost golden and her face smiled a wide strong smile. A loose dress of pastel gold and brown batik complemented her hair and eyes. Her companion was good-looking also, about her age and attired in casual but expensive khaki trousers and matching shirt. My gaydar immediately told me he was gay. They were a handsome couple.

She approached and smiled. "May we join you? You seem to have the only bench with room for others."

"By all means," I said, making space for them. "It looks like it may be a while before we make it through the mob at the counter."

They introduced themselves as Janine and Scott. I told them my name. They said they were New Yorkers, as I suspected from Scott's speech.

"And what brings you to Burma?" I asked when our conversation reached a lull.

"We're on a trip around the world," said Janine. "We needed a break from New York and some of its memo-ries." Scott reached over and lightly squeezed her hand. "And how about you? Why Burma?"

"Curiosity. I've seen most of Southeast Asia, but Burma was pretty much off-limits until recently. I decided to take a look in case it closes its doors again."

"We know little about Burma," admitted Janine. "Our travel agent told us it recently opened to tourists and she thought we would enjoy it. So here we are." She shrugged and smiled. "What do you do back home?"

"I teach anthropology at one of the universities."

"I teach too," said Scott. "Theater at NYU."

"And you?" I asked Janine.

She laughed. "I try to make a living singing opera."

"Don't be fooled by her modesty," said Scott. "She has a marvelous voice and sings frequently at the Met."

"I'm impressed," I said, honestly. "I saw a production of *Lohengrin* at the Met shortly before leaving on this trip. Were you in it by any chance?"

She smiled. "I'm afraid not. I don't do Wagner any more. You'll more likely find me in Puccini or Verdi these days."

"Some of my favorite arias are from Puccini and Verdi. Do you have a favorite?"

She didn't hesitate. "'*Un bel di*' from *Madama Butterfly* when Cio-Cio San is waiting for her lover to return. It was my son's favorite and I often sang it to him as a lullaby. There are many others, of course." She surveyed the room and said, "I'm fearful of what I might find, but I need to use the ladies' room. Do you see it?"

We looked around the room. Scott announced, "It's behind us, beside that tired-looking potted palm."

Janine stood and said, "I'll be right back."

After she left, I said to Scott, "I'd love to hear her sing."

"She's marvelous. Not quite up there with the super-stars, but directly beneath them. If it weren't for the toll her personal tragedies have taken, she'd probably be one of the great contemporary divas."

"What tragedies?" I asked.

Scott paused and then said, "I'm not gossiping. It's common knowledge in the opera world. Her husband died in a car accident about three years ago. They had a beautiful marriage and she was shattered by his death. Two years later her only child committed suicide. He was only seventeen. She never recovered and probably never will. That's one reason we're taking this trip, to be away from New York on the anniversary of his death."

"I'm so sorry. Why did he do it?"

"Who knows? Maybe drugs were involved. Does anyone ever know why someone commits suicide?"

"Perhaps not," I admitted. "She's fortunate to have a friend like you."

"I'm the fortunate one. She's a lovely lady." He paused. "Tomorrow's the anniversary of her son's death."

Janine emerged from the ladies' room and rejoined us. "I need a shower after that," she laughed. "I've never been assaulted by anything so vile. I don't think that room's been cleaned since it was built."

"Welcome to the Third World," said Scott.

We settled into a comfortable silence as we watched the crowd around the counter vie for positions in the nonexistent line. When the crowd thinned, we mutually agreed it was time to face the ordeal. It went surprisingly smoothly and before long our passports were stamped and we exchanged some dollars for *kyat*. After discovering we were staying at the same hotel, we decided to share a cab to Rangoon. A young Burmese man approached and offered to take us to our hotel at a price we thought was reasonable, although we later learned it was about three times that normally charged. We settled into the ancient car that seemed held together with rusty wire and the Buddhist mantra posted above the windshield. As we sped down the rut-ridden road, I could see the pavement through holes in the floor. A sharp turn threw the driver's door open, but fortunately he didn't fall out.

We arrived at the Inya Lake Hotel and discovered rooms awaiting us in that crumbling Soviet-style edifice. After exchanging tired good nights, we were escorted to our separate rooms by quiet young men in wrinkled once-white suits. Janine and Scott followed one of them to rooms on the second floor and I continued to the third floor behind my escort. I refused a suite that featured a giant termite mound in the sitting room and was shown a smaller room with broken windows. I asked for still another room and after witnessing a maid slaughter a rat in the hallway, I settled for a seemingly rat-free, termite-free windowed room with a balcony overlooking the weed-choked lake. Exhausted, I fell into the musty bed and slept a dreamless sleep until awakened by a brilliant sun.

After a tepid shower of brown water that looked and felt like it came directly from the Irrawaddy River, I found my way to the dining room where three guests were unhappily appraising the plates before them. I ordered an English breakfast, an entrée apparently left over from Burma's colonial past. It turned out to be rather good. When I entered the lobby, I saw the couple I met at the airport. We exchanged pleasantries and I continued to the counter where I joined a tour of the city.

Beyond the magnificent Shwedagon Pagoda, most of the places we visited were only mildly interesting. The military presence we encountered almost everywhere prohibited our approach to several of the more promising sites. As usual, I found the people on the streets of greatest interest, including the omnipresent Buddhist monks in their saffron robes. We concluded the tour with a visit to Rangoon's main market, a fascinating place where one could spend days wandering its aisles and exploring its stalls.

That evening I entered the sparsely inhabited hotel dining room and discovered Janine and Scott sitting at a window overlooking the lake. When I approached them, Janine said, "Would you care to join us? We haven't ordered yet."

"Thank you. I'd like that very much. I'm exhausted after my city tour." I sat between them.

"We toured the city also," said Janine. "Too bad we couldn't have seen it together."

"We visited the zoo," said Scott. "The poor animals looked ancient and hungry. I was tempted to set them free."

A waiter appeared for our order and when he departed, we talked more about our tours. They were pleasant, bright people and I enjoyed their company as we ate our way through an unremarkable dinner. Scott dominated the conversation whereas Janine seemed somewhat withdrawn, not the vivacious woman I'd met the day before. Then I remembered this was the anniversary of her son's death. We were all tired from the long day of sightseeing so we parted for our respective rooms after coffee.

I read for about an hour in my room and then extinguished my light. The large sliding door onto the balcony fortunately had an intact screen and the light breeze blowing through it was refreshing after the hot day. I lay in the darkness digesting my book and the day's tour when I heard someone open a door and step onto the balcony below me. Silence followed, interrupted only by the mournful calls of a nocturnal bird. As I wondered what kind of bird would be awake so late, the poignant aria from *Madama Butterfly* softly entered the night on a lovely soprano voice:

> *Un bel di, vedremo*
> *Levarsi un fil di fumo sull'estremo*
> *Confin del mare.*
> *E poi la nave appare.*

The singing ended abruptly in muffled sobs followed by several minutes of quiet crying. After a long silence, the door below me opened once again and then closed. Somewhere in the darkness the nocturnal bird resumed its doleful song.

I left Burma three days later without seeing Janine and Scott again.

Night Train

THE LIGHT BUT persistent rain arrived in early evening and settled in for the night. I sat at a large window in the hotel dining room enjoying a late dinner and watching the people of Prague rush through the rain to evening appointments. It was the end of my stay and with considerable reluctance I was leaving that beautiful museum-like city. But I was looking forward to the next leg of my trip, an overnight train ride to Berlin where I would join an American friend. The Iron Curtain had fallen the previous year and I was visiting some of the newly accessible countries of Eastern Europe. I was traveling alone. I'd shared my train compartments with an assortment of pleasant and not-so-pleasant people and although I was enjoying my solitary journey, I looked forward to joining my friend.

I paid my bill, calculated an appropriate tip and approached the hotel desk where I claimed the piece of luggage I'd left there. The doorman hailed a cab for me and within minutes, I arrived at the train station. I purchased a ticket and searched the departure schedule for my train's platform. I walked down the wet platform and found my car. I entered and discovered that most of the compartments were occupied, dashing my hope that I would have one to myself for the overnight train trip. I found my surprisingly empty compartment. I tossed my bag into the overhead rack and settled into a window seat.

Outside, the rain peppered my window and ran down in little rivulets. Rain had punctuated much of my travels during the past two weeks but it was not an unpleasant rain. I enjoyed watching the land come alive with the warm spring rains. A vibrant green covered the countryside. Lilacs, forsythia and tulips added splashes of color and made me homesick for the Iowa springs of my youth. After many years in the tropics, I was ready to return to temperate climates. Perhaps that was why I felt so comfortable in Europe this trip.

I glanced at my watch. Twenty more minutes before departure. If I were lucky, I'd have the compartment to myself, although that seemed unlikely judging by the number of people on the platform.

The door slid open and I looked up to see a tall, good-looking young man dressed in cowboy attire. He nodded, tossed his backpack into the overhead rack and sat across from me beside the door. He propped his booted feet on the opposite seat, slouched, pulled his cowboy hat over his eyes and folded his arms across his chest. His denim jacket, blue jeans and plaid shirt were worn and wrinkled. He smelled of cigarettes and stale beer. A grubby, wannabe cowboy from America wasn't the companion I had in mind for the trip.

Several minutes later the door slid open again and a dark-haired young man appeared. The dozing cowboy's legs blocked his entrance.

"Excuse me," said the newcomer in American English. The cowboy didn't move.

"Excuse me," he said louder, nudging the cowboy's leg with his canvas bag.

"*Bitte entschuldigen Sie*," said the cowboy, jumping up. I realized for the first time that he was German.

The dark-haired youth glared at him, tossed his bag into the overhead rack and sat opposite him. I smiled at him. He didn't return my smile. He pulled a ragged paperback from his jacket pocket and began reading.

I returned to the activities on the platform where the rain was falling heavier and the people moving faster. A plumpish, sixtyish woman rushed by in a pink plastic raincoat carrying two large canvas bags. She peered at the car and hurried out of sight. Minutes later, the compartment door opened again. The woman in the pink raincoat stood at the entrance.

"I'm afraid I'm in this compartment," she smiled apologetically.

"May I help you with your bags?" I asked, standing up.

"That would be very kind of you." Her English was American.

I took one of her bags and the German youth stood to take the other. We placed them in the rack above us.

"Thank you," she said, smilingly. "So kind of you."

The German murmured something I didn't understand.

As she settled into the window seat opposite me, the train pulled from the platform. We left the station, picked up speed and moved through the dreary suburban apartment complexes that surround Prague's beautiful old city. I caught glimpses of people in lighted windows and imagined domestic dramas. Eventually the suburbs gave way to countryside and only occasional lights from farmsteads interrupted the darkness.

I turned from the window and looked again at my compartment mates. The woman was gazing out the window. A smile played on her lips. The dark-haired youth was still reading. The German, slumped in his seat, was sleeping again.

The woman turned from the window and asked me, "Are you traveling to Berlin?"

"Yes," I replied. "And you?"

"Berlin, also. My husband is meeting me there. Then we're going on to St. Petersburg."

"Are you from America?" I asked.

"Yes. Chicago. And you?"

"San Francisco."

"A beautiful city. My daughter lives there. We visit her each year."

She told me the neighborhood where her daughter lived and about her three grandchildren. As we talked, the dark-haired youth periodically looked up unpleasantly from his book, obviously wanting us to stop talking. The German stirred from his sleep and sat up in his seat.

"You are Americans?" he asked. His accent was very strong and his sentence construction sometimes awkward, but his English was understandable.

"We are," I said. "And you?"

"I am East German," he smiled. "Actually I'm German now. We are one Germany now."

The dark-haired youth glanced at him icily. The woman asked him, "Are you American?"

"I am a Jew."

"But from where?" she asked.

"I've been in Israel for a year. I'm from Philadelphia, but I plan to immigrate to Israel."

"Don't you like America?" she asked.

"I like Israel better."

"What brings you to Europe?"

"To visit the graves of my people who were murdered by a unified Germany." He looked at the German, challenging him to respond. The German appeared embarrassed and said nothing.

"That was another generation. That Germany doesn't exist anymore," said the woman.

"Oh yeah? Tell it to the Turks and Gypsies who get beat up by Nazi punks in Berlin." He looked at the German and returned to his book.

"Are you a student?" I asked the German, changing the conversation to something less loaded.

"No. I organize concerts."

"What kind of concerts?"

"Country-western music concerts. My partner and I book concerts throughout Eastern Europe. The music is very popular here."

"Oh dear," said the woman. "I had no idea you liked that kind of music over here. Were you able to hear that music during the Communist regime?"

"Sure. We got records on the black market. We saw programs on West German TV channels. I never watched that propaganda on our stations."

"So you knew what was happening in the rest of Europe?"

"Of course. I never believed the crap they fed us. They told us all Americans were evil capitalists. You don't look evil to me."

"And you don't look like a dirty Commie," I added.

"Maybe a little dirty," he laughed, looking down at his soiled clothes. "But not a Commie. My friends in Prague gave me a going-away party that lasted all night and most of today. I didn't have time to change."

"Then you were happy to see the end of Communism," said the woman.

"Of course."

"It'll be interesting to see what evolves from a reunified Germany," I said. "I'm sure you know that much of Europe is concerned about a larger, stronger Germany."

"I understand," he said.

"Europe has every right to fear Germany," said the Jewish youth, putting his book aside. "Nothing in Germany's past warrants trust."

"Not all of Germany's past has been bad," said the German.

"You're talking to the wrong person."

"I understand your feelings," said the woman to the Jewish youth. "But you can't blame this young man for his country's past. He was born long after Hitler died."

"All of my father's family was killed at Auschwitz. Germany killed them. German culture is what can't be trusted. And German people are products of German culture. The culture that produced Hitler is alive and well in Germany."

"I don't think it's that simple," said the woman. "Historical events are the result of a unique configuration of episodes at a particular time and place, never to be exactly duplicated. I agree that much of the culture that produced Hitler is still in Germany, but much of it is not. And the special events that brought about Hitler's rise will not happen again. Not to mention there is no Hitler now." She looked at me and said, "Do you agree?"

I was reluctant to enter the heated discussion, but after a long pause I said, "I'm afraid I have a rather low opinion of humankind. Given the right circumstances, I think many people could behave toward another people as the Germans behaved toward the Jews. Look at the European settlers' treatment of American Indians, the annihilation of the Tasmanians. Remember the Khmer Rouge in Cambodia? The Armenians? We call them 'aberrations'—but how many aberrations must occur before we admit they are part of the norm? But I share your view that this young man is blameless for his country's actions before he was born. I don't believe in collective guilt, but I do believe in collective responsibility. Like all of us, he has a responsibility to prevent such things from happening again."

The woman looked at the Jewish youth. "Do you take responsibility for all the things the Jews have done in their past?"

"Of course," he said. "There's nothing in the Jewish past I'm ashamed of."

"I suspect if you looked a little closer at that history, you'd find a few events that are less than noble."

"They wilt compared to the German atrocities."

"Perhaps," she continued. "But carrying hatred from generation to generation solves nothing."

"I've always felt great shame and sorrow at what happened to the Jews," said the German.

"Spare me," said the Jew. He gave the German a withering look and returned to his book.

The woman looked at him and shook her head sorrowfully. "You shouldn't take it personally," she said to the German.

"I can appreciate his feelings."

"What part of East Germany are you from?" she asked.

"Dresden."

"Do your parents still live there?"

"No, my parents are dead. They were both executed when I was six."

"I'm so sorry," said the woman. She paused. "May I ask why they were executed?"

"They were considered enemies of the state. They didn't approve of the Communist regime and tried to sabotage it. They were killed with six others."

"They must be heroes now," I said.

"They were always heroes to me. I'm very proud of them. I was raised by my father's sister who taught me to be proud of my parents."

"A strong Germany could be such a positive influence in Europe," said the woman.

"Yes, it could be," said the German, "but I understand some people's apprehension."

"We can only hope for the best."

The German turned off the light above him, propped his feet on the opposite seat beside the Jewish youth, folded his arms across his chest and closed his eyes. The Jewish youth propped his feet on the seat beside the German and continued reading. The woman and I turned out our lights. She settled into a comfortable position and closed her eyes. I turned to watch the dark forms of the countryside slide past the train.

Throughout this trip, I was reminded of the Holocaust and the conversation of my compartment mates brought back the memories—the Anne Frank house in Amsterdam, a bombed-out synagogue in East Berlin, an untended Jewish cemetery in Vienna and the prison camp at Dachau that I declined to visit. As a child during World War II, I was weaned on anti-Nazi propaganda and spent a good deal of my adulthood overcoming a prejudice against things German. Many of the suspicions, fears and hatreds of the war were very much alive in Europe. Some were voiced this evening.

I settled into a more comfortable position and glanced at the two sleeping youths. Each was stretched out with feet propped on the opposite seat and each had a hand resting on the other's shin. At least they can be friends in sleep, I thought as I closed my eyes to join the slumber of the compartment.

I slept an hour or so. The opening of the compartment door awakened me. The German was gone. The Jewish youth stirred. He leaned over, put on his shoes and left.

I looked at my watch. It was two o'clock. The woman across from me sighed and straightened in her seat.

"You're awake too," she said.

"Yes. These seats do not make good beds."

"Where are our companions?" she asked.

"I think they had trouble sleeping also."

"Such anger the Jewish boy has. Anger like that perverts. It can do no good."

"He's young," I said. "And he's apparently seen some grim reminders of the Holocaust on this trip."

"We've all seen reminders." She peered through the window at the darkness and then continued. "I'm a Jew too. I was in Europe during the war."

"Where?"

"Holland."

"You were able to pass?"

"No. We were in hiding the entire war. We were among the lucky ones."

"Where were you hiding?"

"I was very small. Only eight years old. After the Germans invaded Holland, we were rounded up with other Jews." She paused. "Are you sure you want to hear this?"

"If you don't mind telling it."

"I remember it very vividly. My mother and father and my brother. He was two years older than I. We were at the train station. I'm not sure where we were being sent, but I suppose it was to one of the camps. Something exploded in one of the engines. I don't know what it was. Something mechanical, not a bomb. Everyone was distracted. A

Dutch man rushed to my father and told us to follow him. We followed him outside the station and he took us to a barge on one of the canals. He hid us in the barge and it began moving. I remember the shaking of the engine. We arrived somewhere, somewhere very dark. Then we walked a long time through countryside until we reached his house. His wife fed us and fixed places for us to sleep."

"Did your father know the man?" I asked.

"No. That's the beautiful part. He'd never seen us before. He saw us huddled in the train station and he knew what the Germans were doing to Jews. He couldn't allow it to happen without doing something he told us later."

"You were there the entire war?"

"Yes. Hidden in his house. There were others hidden throughout Holland, just like Anne Frank. Even the man's neighbors didn't know. And he lived in a row house with houses attached to either side."

"No one else in the village knew he was hiding you?"

"Not until the end of the war. Once he heard that Germans were coming to search the village for Jews. He hid each of us in a covered wheelbarrow and pushed us to a hiding place two miles away. He made four trips back and forth pushing us in that rickety old wheelbarrow. Such kindness still makes me weep."

I could hear her sniffling in the dark. "I'm sorry," I said.

"Oh please, don't be sorry. Be happy there was such a man. As horrible as the war was—and it was unspeakably horrible—I always remember the kindness of that man and his family. They had so little food, but they always shared it. There were acts of evil beyond belief during those years, but there were also acts of kindness beyond belief. I was lucky to know some of the kind acts."

"Have you kept in touch with the family?"

"Oh, yes. The parents are dead now, but their children are alive. We spent time with them in Amsterdam a few weeks ago. They are like family to us. They have visited me and my brother several times in America."

"Is your husband American?"

"He is now. Like me, he was born in Germany. His family was not so fortunate. After *Kristallnacht*, his mother feared what would happen next. His father was arrested that night and his mother decided to send my husband and his sister out of Germany. He was only seven and his sister was three. His mother didn't want to leave until she'd made every effort to get her husband out of prison. She heard that a group of Jews were leaving for England, so she went to the train station with the children. They each had a small bag and an address pinned on their coats. The address was a Jewish woman in London who had been a schoolmate of my husband's mother. She approached a Jewish couple who were leaving and asked if they would see that the children made it to the address. Then she left the children."

She stopped, looked out the window and continued. "Imagine that poor woman's desperation. Leaving her two small children with perfect strangers. Not even knowing if her old classmate still lived in London. But she knew she had to get the children out of Germany.

And she was right, of course." She paused. "She and her husband died at Auschwitz."

A long silence followed.

"Did the children reach the woman in London?" I asked.

"Yes, fortunately they did and she raised them as her own. She died last year. A dear woman. My husband and I both loved her very much."

"Another kind soul in all that horror."

"Yes. For me, it's the kind ones who remain in my memory. I know the horror and evil of those days. Believe me, I know. But what remains with me more vividly are the acts of kindness. Perhaps they stand out because they were in the midst of such horror. It gives me faith that there is goodness in humans. Fear, ignorance and perverted politicians cloud and sometimes destroy that goodness. But I think it's always there to be cultivated. Don't you agree?"

"I'm not so sure," I said slowly. "In my darker moods, I'm inclined to believe that cruelty and selfishness are closer to the core of humanity. Cultural traditions do their best to make us otherwise, but when society breaks down and survival is threatened, we sometimes become awful creatures. Goodness and kindness go out the window."

"But we can always see ourselves in one another. Wasn't it John Donne who wrote 'No man is an island'? We need one another for survival. We're social animals. If we had some sort of ingrained fear and dislike of one another we could not survive as a species. Instead, we have this attraction, this need for one another. That I think is what sometimes manifests itself as love."

A small silence stilled our conversation.

"I hope you're right." I stood. "Excuse me. I must find a restroom."

I stepped outside the compartment. The corridor was dark. Small lanterns at either end of the corridor provided the only light. I headed toward the end of the car where I hoped the restroom was located, holding onto the hand-rails to keep my balance as the train clattered through the night. I reached the end of the car and discovered no restroom. I staggered my way to the other end of the darkened corridor. A dim light lit a barely legible sign that told me I'd found a restroom. I opened the door and blinked into the brightly-lighted room. I started.

Inside, the German and Jewish youths were both partly disrobed and wrapped in a tight embrace with their mouths locked together. They jumped apart in alarm. The German reached down to pull up his trousers.

I recovered from my surprise and said, "Excuse me," and closed the door. I stood a moment outside the door and decided to check the adjoining car for a restroom.

When I returned to my car, the Jewish youth was standing at the opposite end of the passage smoking a cigarette and staring through the window into the dark-ness. I entered the compartment and found the German stretched out across the seats. He looked at me sheepishly and moved his legs so I could step past him. The woman was dozing as I settled into my seat. Soon the comforting sound of the softly clattering train lulled me to sleep.

*   *   *

I was the last to awaken in the morning. The woman was leafing through a magazine. The Jewish youth was reading the same ragged book. The German was gazing out the window.

"Looks like I'm the last one up," I said.

The woman smiled. "I envy you. I slept lightly all night long." She turned to look out the window. We were passing through suburban neighborhoods as the sunlight filtered through the grays of early morning.

"We must be nearing Berlin," I said.

"Yes," agreed the German youth. He looked at his watch. "We should arrive at the station in about ten minutes."

"Will you stay in Berlin?" the woman asked him.

"For only three days. Then I go to Paris."

"And you?" she smiled at the Jewish youth who looked up from his book.

"Only long enough to get a train out. I don't feel safe in Germany."

"Nonsense," said the woman. "You're safer here than in most American cities."

"So long as you don't mention you're a Jew."

She looked at him and sighed. "You don't give up, do you? I think you thrive on persecution, both real and imagined."

"Believe me, you don't have to imagine it in Germany. There's plenty of the real stuff around."

"Your hate is as bad as any hate. It only leads to more hate. If people who lived through the Holocaust can put it in the past, why can't you?"

"Maybe I have a perspective they don't have."

"You have no perspective. You're too young. There are many things you cannot begin to understand."

"Spare me the 'wisdom of my elders' speech."

"Someday you'll be embarrassed at what you're saying. Maybe. Maybe not. Some people are fools their entire lives."

"I think we're arriving at the station," I said to change the conversation, but also because we were arriving at the station.

We began collecting our possessions. When the train stopped I stood and lifted the woman's bags from the overhead rack.

The German youth said, "I hope you both enjoy your stay in Berlin. I enjoyed meeting you."

The woman and I returned his good wishes. He looked at the Jewish youth apprehensively. The Jewish youth looked away. The German said "*Auf wiedersehen*," and left the compartment. The Jewish youth pulled his bag down and departed without saying anything.

"Can you handle your bags?" I asked the woman.

"Oh yes. They are bulky but not heavy. I've enjoyed talking with you. May the remainder of your trip be pleasant."

I departed the train and moved down the platform with the early morning crowd toward the lobby of the station. When I stepped outdoors, I was confronted by three young men with shaven heads and swastikas on their armbands. One had a swastika tattooed on his forehead. They shouted loudly as they handed out pamphlets. I understand only a few words of German, but their message was abundantly clear.

Within minutes, policemen arrived and aggressively led them away.

The Survivor

A NNA NAKAMURA WAS one of those little old Japanese women you used to see a lot of in Hawaii. Short and indeterminate of age, they had gray hair, wide smiles and big glasses. Usually wearing housedresses and aprons, they looked like they'd just stepped from an immaculate *Good Housekeeping* kitchen. That was Anna. She was a tiny woman whose smile was ready and generous, but her eyes suggested another story. A touch of sadness never left them. Her husband Yoichi, probably in his early eighties, appeared even smaller than she, possibly because he was bent and scarred by the casualties of age. Her sister Betty, a few years older than Anna, always wore stylish clothes and heavy makeup, reminding me of a tastefully dressed aging hooker. The three lived next door to me in the rural North Shore of Oahu where my partner Matt and I rented a house in the late 1980s. We were both on sabbatical leave from Mainland jobs looking forward to a year in the islands.

One morning I was tackling a patch of stubborn weeds and thinking that maybe we should've opted for a weed-free highrise condo in Waikiki when Anna introduced herself to me at the fence that separated our properties. "Your house has beautiful gardens," she said.

"I'm glad you like them, but at this stage of the game, it's difficult to see much beauty in them. I'm tired of pulling weeds."

She laughed. "I understand. They have a way of getting ahead of you." She lifted a plastic shopping bag from the ground. "I brought you some lychees. They're wonderful this year."

"Thanks so much," I said, accepting the bag and admiring the fruit. "I love lychees. Our tree doesn't seem to have any fruit."

"Your tree is always late. You'll have some later in the season."

"You have beautiful fruit trees on your property," I said.

"Yes, but they need attention. Like us." She laughed. "We planted them many years ago when we first moved here. I'm afraid we're getting too old to give them the proper care they need. It keeps us busy just taking care of ourselves."

"Have you lived out here on the North Shore all your life?"

"Oh no. I was born in a little plantation town on Kauai, but my family moved to Honolulu when I was a teenager in the mid-thirties."

"Then you were in Honolulu during the Pearl Harbor attack?"

"Yes, I was."

"That must have been terrifying."

"Yes it was. Terrible. War is very bad. And where are you from?"

"California. San Francisco. Have you ever been there?"

"No. I was in Southern California during the war, but never in San Francisco."

"You should visit someday. It's a great city."

"That's what everyone tells me, but I haven't been in California since the war ended. I'm too old to travel now. I'll let you get back to your work. I hope you enjoy the lychees."

"I'm sure we will. Thank you very much. And I'm glad I finally met you."

"Same here. Bye."

The lower portion of our property was filled with guava trees and the ground beneath them was carpeted with fallen fruit. About a week after meeting Anna, I picked some of the nicer ones and decided to give them to her—that was before I realized that giving someone in Hawaii a gift of guavas is almost akin to giving an Iowa farmer a gift of corn. I entered her yard and knocked on the front door of the house. Within moments she appeared, wiping her hands on her apron.

"I brought you some guavas," I said.

"Oh, how kind of you," she said graciously. "Won't you come in?"

"Only for a moment. I want to finish some gardening before it becomes too hot."

"I understand," she said as I entered the living room. "I always try to do my outdoor chores in the early morning before it gets hot. My husband is still in bed and my sister is resting. They're not feeling well today. I know they'd both like to meet you. Please sit down." She motioned to a couch. The spotlessly clean room was furnished in styles harking back to the 1950s.

"You have a nice home."

"Thank you," she said. "I'm afraid it's very old-fashioned."

"Nothing wrong with that. It's attractive and very comfortable. That's what's important." I noticed a bookcase filled with photos. "Is that your family," I asked, as I moved to examine the photos more closely.

"Yes, most of them are."

The majority of the photos were children and high school graduates in cap and gown. In one, a much younger pretty Anna and a handsome young Japanese man were seated with two little boys. "Is this your husband and children?" I asked.

"Yes," she said.

"What adorable children. You must be proud of them."

"Yes, I am."

"Do they live in Hawaii?"

"No, they don't."

She obviously wasn't interested in talking about her family, so I changed the subject to a gardening problem I was having with some hibiscus cuttings. She warmed to the subject and offered advice.

A frail male voice called from a nearby room, "Anna. Where is my tea?"

"In a minute, Yoichi. The new neighbor is visiting."

"I told you I was ready for my tea fifteen minutes ago," said the voice irritably.

"I'm sorry," I said. "I'm afraid I'm interrupting your morning." I stood to leave.

"My husband is having a bad day," said Anna apologetically, walking me to the door. "Please come back again when he's feeling better. I'm sure he'd enjoy meeting you. And I know my sister wants to meet you too. Thank you for the lovely guavas."

A week later, I was in the yard assembling a lawn mower I bought in Honolulu to control the grass that seemed to grow an inch each time I turned my back. When I ordered the mower, I assumed it would arrive assembled rather than in the dozen pieces scattered around me. Never a directions-reader, I was trying to do it on my own and growing increasingly frustrated.

I heard a voice from next door: "Hello. You must be the Californian."

I turned and saw an older Japanese woman leaning on the fence. "That's me," I said, happy to take a break from the exasperating assembly job. "And you must be Anna's sister."

"That's me. I'm Betty. I'm the ornery one," she laughed. She was perfectly coiffed, her jet black hair incorporated into a hairpiece pinned atop her head. Her make-up was heavy but carefully applied and her dress looked more appropriate for an evening cocktail party than a morning chat over the fence. She smiled at me mischievously.

"And why are you the ornery one?" I asked, joining her at the fence.

"I was the one with all the boyfriends who liked to party and dance and stay up all night. Anna was always the one who obeyed the rules. So much for obeying the rules—look where it got her. Stuck out here in the country with a cranky old man. I'm stuck out here, too, but at least I have some great memories." She laughed.

"So you're from Kauai too?"

"Can't you tell? When I was young they always said that all the pretty girls came from Kauai." She laughed coquettishly.

"And you're holding up that tradition."

"I bet you say that to all the girls." She feigned modesty, placing a hand over her mouth.

"Only the pretty ones," I said, playing her game. "Have you lived in the islands all your life?"

"Yes. I moved to Honolulu from Kauai, and only came out here when the rents became too high and I was too sick to live alone."

"I'm sorry you're not well. You certainly look very fit." And she did. She was probably in her late sixties, slim and attractive.

"I'm not a well woman." She seemed rather offended that I thought she was healthy. "I've been in the emergency room three times during the past month. I have a very bad heart."

"I'm sorry. I didn't know. Have you lived with your sister very long?"

"Only about a year. I moved out here because I needed Anna's help. I didn't realize that old man would live so long. He takes all her time. I'm much sicker than he is, but he resents me. He's always been that way."

"Do you have children?" I asked, trying to move away from family squabbles.

"No. I never had time for children. Anna had children. I had husbands." She laughed again. "I was married three times and would be looking for number four if I wasn't so sick."

"You never know. He may be around the next corner."

She laughed. "I wish. But I didn't come over to flirt with you. I wanted to ask if our chickens are a nuisance. I noticed some of them in your yard yesterday. We try to keep our fence secure so they can't get loose, but they always seem to find a way out."

"They're no bother," I assured her. "In fact, we rather like them around. I've always liked the clucking of chickens."

"Let us know if they become a problem. I'll give you some eggs for putting up with them."

"That would be great, but there's no need for that."

"Not a problem. We have more eggs than we can use." She coughed lightly. "I must go inside and rest. My chest is beginning to tighten. I feel a little light-headed too." She turned to leave. "It was nice talking to you."

"Thanks for stopping by. I enjoyed meeting you. I hope you feel better soon."

"I'll never feel better again. I don't know what it is to be well. It's something I've learned to live with. I'm a very sick woman. Bye."

I watched her walk to the house. As she entered the front door, she called, "Anna! I need my medicine. Bring it to my bedroom. Make me some tea too.

And don't make it so strong this time. You know I like it weak."

The next morning I gave up on the lawn mower. I finally got it assembled, but it wouldn't start. I decided it was time for some professional help, loaded it into my pick-up and took it down to the local mechanic. His garage was located across the highway from one of the spectacular North Shore beaches. "If you gotta work," I thought to myself, "not a bad place to do it."

The Japanese man who greeted me when I pulled in was not one of the regular mechanics. He knew me however. "You the guy from California?" he asked. I wasn't surprised that he knew me. The North Shore was a small town back then and everyone soon knew everything that happened.

I acknowledged that I was the guy from California.

"You live next to my dad's cousin."

"Anna is his cousin?" I asked.

"No, the grumpy old man Anna has to put up with."

"I haven't met him yet."

"Lucky you," he muttered under his breath. "What can I do for you?"

I explained my lawn mower problem and he said he would take it apart and reassemble it to make sure all the pieces were in the right places. I concurred that it was probably a good idea. He began disassembling the mower.

"Anna is certainly a nice woman," I said, continuing our conversation.

"Yeah, she is. But she's had some hard knocks—including that old man she married. Her sister's no gem either."

"I guess everyone accumulates a few bad knocks during a lifetime."

"Yeah, but some more than others. Do you know her story?"

"No, I don't know a lot about her. Just a couple of chats over the fence with her and her sister."

"Everyone knows it." He paused to loosen a tight bolt. I waited for him to continue. "Old Yoichi is her second husband. Her first husband and her two little boys were killed in the Pearl Harbor attack. One of the bombs hit their house. Fortunate for Anna, she was in town taking care of her mother. She would've been much better off with that first husband than this old fart she's stuck with now."

"That's a horrible story!" I said. "It must have been devastating for her."

"It was. I don't think she ever got over it. But you gotta move on in life. She moved in the wrong direction though when she married again."

A few days later, Matt and I were at the lower end of the property hacking away at the coarse gargantuan grass that grew above our heads—called "California grass" by the locals. I wasn't in Hawaii long before I learned that most things the locals don't like are blamed on California. We collapsed under a tree for a break from the strenuous hot work when we heard a weak voice call, "Please help me."

I stood and listened. Again the voice called, "I fell. Please help me."

"Where are you?" Matt shouted.

"Over here. Under the orange tree." The voice came from Anna's weed-choked orchard. Matt and I pushed our way through the grass and climbed the fence separating our properties.

"Where are you?" Matt shouted again.

"Here," was the reply. "Over here under the orange tree."

We followed the voice through the tangled vegetation to a clearing where a fruit-laden orange tree stood. Beneath it was an old, frail Japanese man lying on his side.

"Are you Anna's husband?" I asked him.

"Yes. I am Yoichi Nakamura."

"What happened?" Matt asked.

"I fell," he said. "I was feeling better today, so I came down to check on the fruit trees. Anna and Betty went to town for groceries. They shouldn't have left me alone. Can you help me back to the house? I think I may have broken something."

We carefully lifted the little old man and carried him up the hill to the house where he directed us to his bedroom. We placed him on the bed.

"Thank you so much," he said. "I'm sorry to trouble you."

"No trouble," I said. "I'm glad we heard your call. Are you in pain? Maybe we should take you to the hospital."

"No, I don't think I could ride in a car. I don't have much pain, but something's wrong with my hip.

Maybe you better call 911 for an ambulance. We've done that before."

"Have you fallen before?"

"No, but for other problems. Usually for Betty. She always thinks she has heart trouble." There wasn't much sympathy in his voice.

I went to the telephone, dialed 911 and told the operator what happened. I gave directions to the house and returned to the bedroom.

"Thank you," said the old man. "It takes them awhile to get here." He rearranged himself on the bed and said: "You're from California aren't you?"

"Yes," I said. "San Francisco."

"I've never been there, but I was in California during the war years. I hated it. Suffocating hot in the summer and cold in the winter."

"Where were you?" I asked.

"Manzanar. Have you ever heard of Manzanar?"

"Yes, of course, I have," I said. "I'm sorry. That must have been a very difficult time for you." The World War II incarceration of Japanese-Americans was currently receiving headlines as the U.S. Congress considered reparations for the survivors. Manzanar and other so-called "relocation camps" were very much in the news.

"Of course, it was. That's where I met Anna. We were married after we were released."

"Anna was at Manzanar?" I asked incredulously. "I thought she was here during the Pearl Harbor attack."

"She was. But when her family was killed, her brother in California talked her into visiting him to get away from her sorrows. Shortly after she arrived there, she was sent to Manzanar with her brother and his family. I was a friend of her brother. "

"That's horrible," I said, genuinely shocked. "The poor woman."

"She wasn't the only one," he said quickly. "It was difficult for all of us. I lost my business and got tuberculosis. I've been sickly ever since. She's always been healthy."

At that point, a car drove up and moments later the front door opened.

"Anna," called the old man. "You're finally back. I fell down."

Anna and Betty came into the bedroom. "What happened?" asked Anna, acknowledging me and Matt.

"I was checking the fruit trees down below and I fell."

"That was a dumb thing to do," said Betty. "You should've known better than walk down that hill."

"I think I broke something."

"Small wonder," said Betty, unsympathetically, and then somewhat hopefully, "Is it serious?"

"I'm in terrible pain. I can't stand it." He told us earlier he had no pain.

"I called 911," I said. "They should be here soon." As if on cue, the ambulance pulled up outside and moments later we heard a knock at the door. Anna ushered in two burly young Hawaiian men. One of them examined the old man. They decided he needed medical attention and went to the ambulance for a stretcher.

"My chest is hurting again," said Betty. "Too much excitement. I'm going to my room and rest. Bring me some tea, Anna."

"In a minute," said Anna, as the paramedics placed her husband on a stretcher.

"You're coming with me, aren't you?" the old man asked Anna.

"I'll follow in the car."

"I shouldn't be left alone," said Betty. "My chest is terribly painful."

"I'll come right back as soon as Yoichi is checked into the hospital."

"If you wish, we can stay with you," I said to Betty.

"Oh no," she said. "I'm accustomed to being ignored and left alone. This is nothing new." She went to her room.

Anna looked at her exasperatedly.

"Is there anything we can do?" I asked her.

"No, no. She'll be alright. I'll be right back. This has all happened before. Thank you for everything you've done." We followed the paramedics outside where Anna watched them load her husband into the ambulance. She then followed them in her car.

I called in the house to ask Betty if she was alright. She assured me she was. Matt and I returned to the lower lot and hacked some more at the stubborn grass. A couple of hours later, we called it a day and stopped by Anna's house to check on events. Anna had left Yoichi in the hospital and Betty was still in bed. Anna assured us she had everything under control and promised to call if she needed any help. Somewhat reluctantly we left her.

Yoichi never returned from the hospital. He suffered a severe stroke the second day he was there and died within a week. And indeed, Betty was not a well woman.

She died of a heart attack about a month after the old man's funeral.

We attended the Buddhist funeral services for each of them. Anna was dressed in black and thanked us for attending. She seemed sad, but no sadder than usual. She shed no tears at the services, nor did anyone else among the small group of friends and family.

Anna continued to live alone in her home. I occasionally saw her gardening outside and talked to her over the fence. I gave her our telephone number and told her to call if she ever needed anything. She thanked me profusely, assuring me she was quite alright. And she did seem alright, if anything stronger and happier. The little cloud of sadness that was always with her had dissipated. She spent a lot of time outdoors with her flowers and her yard became a showpiece of tropical gardening. She slowly but persistently cleared the weeds from the orchard and it too burst with new life. Periodically, she arrived smilingly at the fence or at our door with gifts of flowers from her garden or fruit from her orchard. Once she accepted my invitation to come inside and see the house but otherwise she always declined, claiming she must return to some chore awaiting her at home.

About four months after the deaths of Betty and Yoichi, our sabbaticals ended and Matt and I returned to the Mainland. Anna and I exchanged letters regularly. She increasingly mentioned that the maintenance of her home was becoming difficult for her, so I wasn't too surprised when she told me she was considering selling her house and moving to a nearby assisted-living facility. She wrote me after she moved and expressed happiness at being there. Thereafter, her letters became fewer and briefer. The final one I received was almost unintelligible and barely decipherable. In response to my reply, I received a note from her niece who told me Anna had Alzheimer's disease and was unable to answer my letters. I responded to the niece expressing sorrow at Anna's condition. She answered and thanked me for being a friend to her aunt and that was the end of our correspondence.

About a year later, I returned to Hawaii and decided to visit Anna one day when I was driving out to the North Shore. I was uncertain about her condition and wasn't sure she would remember me but I decided to give it a try. I easily located the nursing home where she was now living. I made my way through an attractively landscaped courtyard populated by several elderly women in wheelchairs. They stared vacantly into space except one who smiled and wished me, "Good morning." I returned her greeting and entered the lobby where I was greeted by a young Hawaiian woman at the reception desk.

"Good morning," I said. "Is Anna Nakamura still living here? I'm an old friend and would like to visit her."

"Yes, Anna is still with us. Have you been in touch with her recently?"

"No, I haven't. I understand she has Alzheimer's."

"She's a very sweet woman, one of our favorite residents. She lives mostly in the past these days so possibly she will remember you. I'll call someone to take you to her."

She pushed buttons and spoke into a speaker asking June to come to the lobby. Within moments, a pleasant matronly Filipina arrived who was informed that I was a friend of Anna. I followed her down an immaculate hallway and glanced into the rooms of the elderly residents. Most were in bed sleeping, some were slumped in wheelchairs staring at nothing.

"Anna has her good and bad days," warned my escort. "She is always very sweet, but some days she has no idea where she is. Other days she lives in the past where she seems happiest. Here she is."

We entered a room where a tiny Japanese woman sat in a rocker, smiling and humming as she gazed out the window.

"Good morning, Anna. You have a visitor. This gentleman used to be your neighbor. Do you remember him?"

Anna turned and smiled at me vacantly. I approached her, took her hand and said, "Hello Anna. Remember me? The Californian who lived next to you in Pupukea?"

"Oh, yes," she said blankly. "How nice of you to come over and visit me. I've intended to have you over for some time. Please have a chair."

"Thank you," I said, sitting on her bed since no chair was available. "How are you?"

She laughed. "Busy as usual. So many things to do this time of year. The fruit is ripening so quickly. I made some mango chutney yesterday. I'll give you a jar when you leave."

"Thank you," I said. "That's very kind of you. I always liked your mango chutney."

"And the boys," she continued. "They're growing so fast I can't keep them in clothes. You won't recognize them. They'll be home from school soon. I hope you can stay long enough to see them. They're doing so well at school. They are such good boys. And so handsome like their father. Noboru will be home soon too. He likes to be here when the boys return from school. I hope you can stay. He'll be upset if he misses you."

"I'd love to see them all, but I can't stay too long."

"Oh I hope you stay long enough to see them. And I want you to have some mangoes. They're so delicious this year and such a bumper crop. I'll have the boys climb the tree and pick some of the beautiful ones I see in the upper branches. They'll love that." Her eyes twinkled. "You know how boys love to climb trees."

She turned away from me and looked out the window, quietly humming a happy tune, smiling and slowly rocking in her chair. She seemed to have forgotten that I was in the room. Then she fell asleep.

I watched her several minutes before retracing my steps to the lobby.

"Is Anna happy today?" asked the woman at the reception desk.

"Yes." I paused a moment, admiring a white orchid on the desk. "Yes, I think Anna is finally happy."

Mabata

NO TWO WAYS about it, Mabata was a gorgeous hunk of a man. And I wasn't the only one who thought so. Everyone who knew Mabata fell in love with him.

I met Mabata at the University of Hawaii in an anthropology class during my first semester there. A Polynesian from the Tuamotu Islands northeast of Tahiti, he was in Hawaii on a university scholarship. Twenty-six years old, he was six feet four, two hundred and twenty pounds with a powerful chest and matching arms and legs. Warm brown eyes and wavy auburn hair complemented his smooth golden skin. His easy smile would melt an iceberg.

The class I shared with Mabata was small and before the semester ended we became good friends. One day after class, I invited him to join me in the student cafeteria for coffee. He politely told me he was a Mormon and didn't drink coffee, but would join me for a non-caffeinated soft drink. He was carrying *The Book of Mormon*.

As we settled into chairs on the patio beside a hibiscus bush bursting with fiery red blossoms, he asked me, "What is your religion?"

I was somewhat taken aback at the personal question, but said, "I don't have any."

He was quiet momentarily and then said, "How is that possible? Everyone has a religion."

"Not me."

"What about your family? Does no one have religion?"

"Most of them don't."

"Where do your people come from?"

"Scotland," I said, "but don't blame the Scots. Most Scots have religion. Is religion important to you?"

"Of course. I am a Mormon."

"And your family?"

"They are Mormons." He paused. "But some of them still have pagan beliefs."

"Such as?"

He thought a moment. "My grandfather sometimes leaves offerings for the old gods. When he goes fishing, he prays to a stone for success. In the old days, my people believed some gods live in stones. Some still believe that."

I glanced at the book on the table. "Why do you carry *The Book of Mormon*?"

"I read it when I have spare time. Some parts I don't understand too well but I must cleanse myself of the old beliefs of my people. I don't believe most of that nonsense anymore, but sometimes I have pagan thoughts. It helps if I read *The Book of Mormon*. I worked with Mormon missionaries back home and they helped clean my soul of the old pagan ways."

I have trouble with the cleansing power of Christianity, or any other proselytizing religion for that matter, so I changed the subject to an upcoming exam.

One day after class, Mabata asked if I'd accompany him to Queen's Surf Beach the following Saturday. In those days, Queen's Surf was about the only beach in Waikiki frequented by locals. Part of its popularity stemmed from the three bars housed in a Mediterranean-style building facing a wide expanse of white sand that dipped into the Pacific Ocean. It was becoming a hangout for gays who had great fun with its name. I'm not a big beach person but I agreed to go, partly because I wanted to see if Mabata's body was as magnificent disrobed as it was robed. I wasn't disappointed. When he stripped to his swim trunks, a Polynesian Adonis emerged. Every eye on the beach checked him out but he was oblivious to the attention he was garnering. Feeling somewhat like the "before" photo in a Charles Atlas ad, I unrolled my beach mat and prepared to soak up some midday rays. We talked about our class and discussed possible term paper topics.

"Why did you decide to study anthropology?" I asked during a pause in our conversation.

"So I can help my people change and take advantage of the modern world. Many of them still live primitive lives in darkness with their old religion."

"Why didn't you become a missionary?"

He hesitated. "I thought about it once."

"And what changed your mind?"

He thought for a moment. "Some missionaries are good, but many have no respect for the old ways. They think they're all bad. But they're not all bad. Some are good—like how we care for our families, the way we respect our old people, the good times we have at our celebrations."

I noticed since his disrobing, a large pendant hanging around his neck. "What is your pendant? It's very impressive. May I look at it?"

"Of course, but I cannot take it off." He leaned over so I could examine it.

Ivory-colored and the size of a small egg, the pendant was incised with abstract symbols.

"What are the symbols?"

"My family's carvings. They have *mana* which protects me. It was made by my ancestor from a whale's tooth. We are related to the whale. My grandfather gave it to me when I left home."

"So you believe in some of the old ways too?"

He blushed slightly and seemed embarrassed. "I wear it in respect for my grandfather and my ancestors. We can respect the old and still embrace the new. But we need to make some changes, like better medicine and healthier diets."

"And you think you can do that as an anthropologist?"

"Yes. I worked with an anthropologist who did fieldwork on our island when I was still a student there." He named him. I knew his work. "That's how I learned about anthropology. We talked about changes that could improve my people's lives. And he's the one who told me about the scholarship at the university."

"So you plan to return home after you finish your degree?"

"Of course. What else would I do? That's where my family is. All my ancestors are buried there. Of course, I'll go home."

The semester ended. I didn't have any more classes with Mabata, but I frequently saw him on campus and we occasionally caught a movie together or spent an afternoon at the beach. The following summer I ran into him after not seeing him for several weeks. He invited me to join him at the cafeteria. When we sat down with our trays, I noticed he had a Coke, something he declined on other occasions because of the caffeine tabooed by his Mormon religion. I didn't say anything.

"Are you still living at the same place?" he asked, taking a long drink of his Coke.

"Yep. Same old cockroach motel."

"My roommate's moving out in late August," he said. "I can't afford the apartment by myself. Would you like to move in? There are two bedrooms. I don't want to advertise for a roommate and have some stranger move in. I think you'd make a good roommate."

We discussed the rent and I learned that his apartment was closer to campus than my grungy digs. "Let me think about it," I said. "I'll get back to you in a few days."

After some serious thought, I decided to move in with Mabata. By now, I was accustomed to his beauty and thought he was straight, so I knew sex wouldn't mess up our friendship. I visited his apartment, liked what I saw and agreed to move in when his roommate left in late summer.

Honolulu was abuzz that summer with news and gossip about Hollywood people in town to cast a movie based on a currently popular best-selling novel about the islands. Three of Hollywood's top stars had the major roles, but the lesser ones were being filled with local talent. Consequently all the island hams appeared for tryouts at the Hilton Hotel in Waikiki. One of the roles they hoped to fill locally was that of a good-looking pre-European Hawaiian chief. And guess what? Mabata got the role. I'm not sure how they found him or how he found them, but if the word was out that they were looking for a good-looking, hunky Polynesian man, many people would have recommended Mabata. I read in the paper that he was offered the role. The following evening I was taking a break from a boring article I was reading for a seminar when the telephone rang. I picked up the receiver.

"Hello, this is Mabata."

"Hey, Mabata. Good to hear from you. Congratulations. I heard that you got a role in the big movie."

"Thanks. Yes, I did. It was totally unexpected. I was walking in Waikiki with a friend when two guys came up and asked if I'd like to try out for the role. I said sure, why not? I went to the hotel, read the script and they told me the part was mine. They'll pay me to take acting lessons and then I'll be ready to go."

"Do you have an agent?"

"Yes and I've already signed a contract. It's a lot of money. I can buy many things for my family."

"That's wonderful, Mabata. I'm really pleased for you."

"Thank you. I'm happy too." He paused. "I'm going to Hollywood for the acting lessons. That's one reason I called. After Hollywood, we'll go to Tahiti to film for several months. I'm not sure when I'll be back so I thought it best if I give up my apartment. Will this cause you problems?"

"No, not at all. I haven't given notice yet. I can stay here. No problem."

"Thanks for understanding. I'll be able to go home and see my family when we finish in Tahiti. I'm very excited." He paused. "But I'm not giving up anthropology. I still want to finish my degree."

"I'm sure you will, Mabata. This is a chance of a lifetime. Who knows what it might lead to? Even if it goes nowhere, it'll be great experience for you and a chance to earn some extra bucks."

"That's exactly what I thought. Thanks for understanding."

I didn't see Mabata before he left for Tahiti, but since some scenes of the movie were filmed in Hawaii and many local people had roles, the newspapers covered its progress. Occasionally Mabata's name was mentioned, but mostly it was the big stars and the better-known local talent who got the press coverage. I was preparing for my PhD exams and didn't have a lot of time to think about Mabata or anything else non-anthropological.

During the second semester of that year, a professor and his wife who befriended me shortly after I arrived in the islands asked if I'd house-sit for them while they were on sabbatical leave in Japan. I jumped at the chance to escape the confines of my grubby little apartment for the spacious coolness of their big home in Manoa Valley. I was about two months into my house-sitting when some friends talked me into throwing a party. I'd just passed my PhD exams and had reason for celebration. Word got out about the party and a big crowd showed up. Several times during the course of the evening, I cursed myself for letting the party get so big. At one time I counted almost a hundred people, many of whom I didn't know. As I was mopping up some spilled beer from the kitchen floor someone called my name. I looked up and saw Mabata. I almost didn't recognize him.

"Mabata!" I said. "Good to see you!"

He squeezed me in a big bear hug, a considerable departure from the formal handshake he normally offered. His hair was almost shoulder-length and he was either growing a beard or hadn't got around to shaving the past week or two. He wore ragged blue jeans and sandals with a faded shirt open to his waist which showed off his great chest. Around his neck was the whale tooth pendant. He held a can of beer.

"How's the movie going?" I shouted over the din of the party.

"Almost finished," he shouted back. "We're wrapping it up here in Hawaii. Let's go outside so we can talk easier."

"Good idea." I led him outside onto a lanai which was empty except for a stranger passed out in a chair.

"So how do you like the Hollywood life?"

"It's been good," he said. "I've met some great people. And a few who aren't so great."

"Pretty much the way people are."

"After we finished filming in Tahiti, I went home and saw my family. They had a big party for me. The whole island was there."

I couldn't resist asking, "I see you're drinking beer. What do your Mormon friends think about that?"

"I don't know. I don't see them anymore. I'm no longer a Mormon."

"What happened?"

"The Mormon religion is okay for white people, but when I returned home, I realized that my ancestors' religion is for me. My grandfather was so happy when I told him. He was afraid I would never come back."

"And what happens when the movie is over?"

"My agent thinks I can make a good living in movies and television. I enjoy the life. And the money is good." He added hastily, "But I plan to return to school. I still want to become an anthropologist and go home and help my people. But for a few years, I'll work in movies. Next week I'm going to Hollywood and audition for a part. My agent thinks I'll get it."

"What's the movie?"

He told me what he knew about the film, a thriller set in Asia at the court of a nineteenth century potentate, the role he was auditioning for. Our conversation wandered to mutual acquaintances and we eventually rejoined the party.

I left Hawaii for a couple of years of fieldwork in the southern Philippines and didn't hear much about Mabata. The Hawaii film was released while I was overseas and I read a lukewarm review of it in *Newsweek*. Mabata received a positive review, but the reviewer seemed most impressed by his gorgeous body and good looks and hardly noted his acting. A few months later, a friend wrote me and told me he'd seen Mabata in a television drama where he played a Burmese prince who smuggled jewels into California. The writers apparently didn't realize, or weren't concerned, that Mabata was about twice the size of most Burmese men.

I returned to Hawaii, finished my PhD and took a teaching job in San Francisco. During my first month there, Mabata's most recent film was released. This one was based on a historical account of a massacre of Lakota Indians during the mid-nineteenth century. Mabata played a handsome young brave who tried to bridge understanding between his people and the invading whites. It was the first time I'd seen Mabata act and he seemed rather wooden to me. But the whole movie was such a cliché that it was difficult to judge the acting. Mabata didn't say, "Ugh. Me redskin Indian," but some of his lines were close. But who cares about acting when there's Mabata to look at? Apparently the critics did. The film was roundly panned.

* * *

About ten years later I hooked up with Mabata again. His bit parts in films continued and occasionally I caught him on television shows, especially a detective series set in Hawaii. I heard that he appeared in television commercials, but I never saw them. He usually played an Indian, a Polynesian or some undefined ethnic type from an even less-defined part of the Third World. To my knowledge he never had a major role, but he appeared in a couple of box office successes. His acting never set the world on fire, but some people probably remember him because of his great looks.

I was living in San Francisco when a friend called one day and invited me to join her to see a new musical headed for Broadway at a local theater. I like good musical theater, but this one with a cowboy western setting didn't appeal to me. I tried to beg off, but my friend insisted she had no one else to accompany her so I caved in.

We met at a downtown restaurant and walked to the theater after dinner. As the overture unfolded, I recognized some of the songs resurrected for the musical. The curtain went up and the act began none-too-promising as an aging, once big-time actress opened her pipes for the first song. The silly, predictable plot plodded on, relieved only by an occasional good song. A long day on campus was about to close my eyes when loud yelps from the stage awakened me as a group of "Indians" invaded the action. Dressed in Hollywood-Indian style, they epitomized the racist stereotyping of Indians that dominated the screen for the first fifty-plus years of Hollywood's existence. Political correctness had not dictated some much needed rewriting. As I watched the embarrassing caricatures on stage, I suddenly realized the man playing the Indian chief was none other than Mabata! I was embarrassed for him. I expected radical Indians to invade the theater and close down the production. Such didn't happen, however, and the show reached its tired conclusion. I told my friend that I knew Mabata and wanted to go backstage to say hello. She was enthusiastic.

We made our way backstage and were directed to an area where we could await the actors as they left the theater. They wandered out in pairs and small groups, and then Mabata appeared. He immediately recognized me as a broad smile overtook his face. He rushed to me and embraced me warmly.

"It's so damn good to see you," he said. "Where have you been all these years?"

"Like you, here and there." I introduced him to my friend.

"Do you live here in San Francisco?" he asked. Several other cast members were standing in the background, obviously waiting for him.

"Yes, I've been here since I left Hawaii. I've seen you on television and in movies, but never knew where you were living."

"I divide my time between Hollywood and New York." He glanced at the waiting cast members. "My friends are waiting for me to join them. Can I call you? Let's have dinner and talk over old times."

"I'd like that." We exchanged telephone numbers and after another big hug, he left with his companions.

"God, what a gorgeous man!" drooled my friend.

True to his word, Mabata called me the next morning and we made a dinner date for the following Monday, dark night at the theater. I suggested an Italian place on upper Market Street that he could easily reach by street-car. I arrived a bit early and was chatting with the owner of the restaurant when Mabata appeared.

"Good to see you," I said, holding out my hand which he ignored in favor of a hug.

"I'm glad you came backstage. I had no idea you lived here in San Francisco."

"And I had no idea you were in this musical. I was there by chance. My friend had an extra ticket."

"It's not very good, is it?" he said, as we sat at our table.

"Some of it's a little dated," I suggested diplomatically. "But many of the musical numbers are good."

He made a face. "I'm surprised some of the Native American activists haven't shut us down."

"It's a little heavy on stereotypes."

"More than heavy. The only reason I took the role was the money. No jobs were beating down my door, so I decided to join their road show. It's on its way to Broadway, but I doubt if it ever gets there."

We gave our orders to a hovering waiter.

"Now, tell me about your career. I've seen you in a few movies and you keep popping up on television. Is the movie world as glamorous as they'd like us to believe?"

"I'm not sure 'glamorous' is the word I'd use. It's okay. It sometimes pays well. I've been able to give my family a good life back home."

"Where's your home base?"

"I have a place in L.A. and another in New York. Most of my work is out of those two places. The one in New York isn't my own. I live with a woman doctor when I'm there. I have my own apartment in L.A."

"And a woman there?"

He smiled. "Let's say I don't get lonely."

Mabata was watching the parade of gay men passing our window and asked, "Is this the gay part of the city?"

"Yep. We're only a block from the Castro, the heart of gay San Francisco."

"You're gay, aren't you?" he said matter-of-factly.

"When did you figure that out?"

"I guess I always suspected it. It's no issue for me. I've never understood all the fuss about gay in this country. I enjoy sex with men, but I like women too. Why does one have to rule out the other?"

"I guess it doesn't if you get pleasure from both and no one gets hurt."

The waiter arrived with our dinners. "I finished my degree in anthro at Hawaii," Mabata announced proudly as he dug into his pasta. "I took classes when I was over there for shoots and eventually I graduated. That was important for me."

"I'm glad. I remember you always wanted to finish your degree and help your people."

"And I did."

"I bet they're very grateful to you."

"I think they are. They think I'm a famous movie star. I tell them I'm just a bit player, but they don't want to hear it. It doesn't matter to me."

I watched him eat. He'd put on some weight since our years together in Hawaii, but he was still a fabulous looking man. More than one gay head passing our window spun for a double-take.

"Do you live near here?" he asked.

"Yeah. I have a flat a couple blocks away."

"I'd like to see it." He looked up and smiled.

I almost choked on my wine. Was this a proposition? "It's nothing special, but I'd be happy to show it to you."

We finished dinner and were nursing the last of the wine when Mabata asked "Shall we go?"

I won't dwell on the details. We went to my flat and almost before the front door closed we were in bed. I've had my fair share of sexual partners and I can say with confidence that few of them vie with Mabata.

We lay in bed and talked in the afterglow.

"So do you still like acting?" I asked him.

"It has its moments. But it's mostly the money that keeps me in it. I've been able to put aside trusts for my children."

"Children? I didn't know you were married. When did that happen?"

"I've always been married since you've known me. My wife never left the Tuamotus where my children are."

I was flabbergasted. "I had no idea. How many children do you have?"

"Three at last count."

"Have they ever visited you here in the States?"

"The two older ones were here. They didn't care much for it. The younger one isn't interested in coming. I go home at least once a year and see them."

"And your wife? She's never been here?"

"No. She has absolutely no interest in coming."

"Do your girlfriends know about your wife and kids?"

"Of course. I would never lie about that. I'm proud of them."

Mabata slept over and after a leisurely breakfast, he left in the morning. His show closed the following weekend and moved on to Seattle. I didn't see him again before he left town.

I've traveled a good portion of the globe, but I'd never visited Polynesia beyond Hawaii which was somewhat ironic since that part of the world initially attracted me to anthropology. A few years ago, my partner Matt and I decided to take a leisurely swing through the islands of the South Pacific. We worked out a great itinerary that included the Galapagos, Rapa Nui, Tahiti, Samoa, Fiji, Vanuatu, Port Moresby and on to Sydney and back to San Francisco—a big swath across the southern Pacific.

As I plowed through travel books and maps of the region, I remembered Mabata and the Tuamotu Islands. I hadn't heard about him in years. I wasn't even sure he was still alive, quite a number of old friends had exited in recent years. I went online to see if I could find something about him, but all I pulled up were references to his films. I emailed a few old friends but they knew nothing about him.

We flew to Santiago. A day later, we continued on to Rapa Nui and explored that island for several days. Although I knew a lot about Rapa Nui, I was nonetheless awed by those huge stone statues that were erected and then toppled by that deviant Polynesian population on their little speck of land. We flew on across the Pacific to Tahiti where we planned to stay perhaps a week, our itinerary was flexible.

I won't try to write about the beauty of Tahiti. I can add little to the volumes already written about that legendary island and its lovely satellites. Suffice it to say that Tahiti didn't disappoint me. We checked into a Papeete hotel in early afternoon and decided on a nap after the long flight.

I awoke late afternoon and went downstairs to the lounge where Matt was waiting with a frosty beer. I ordered a gin and tonic in my fractured French as we plotted our next move. After drinks, we decided to wander the waterfront, a place that always fascinates me wherever I travel. The sun was less intense, but still hot when we left the hotel and joined the throng on the busy street that fronted the harbor. An array of watercraft filled the water, all overshadowed by a French luxury liner that docked that afternoon. We sat on a bench and watched the lively activities.

A very large, older Polynesian man approached, looked at me keenly and then said in English, "Could you possibly be . . . ?"

"Mabata!" I cried, jumping up and embracing my old friend. "I didn't know you were in Tahiti."

"And I never expected to find you here!" He embraced me again, crunching me in his bulk. He had gained at least fifty pounds since I last saw him, probably more. He was still a good-looking man. He wore a sarong and loose aloha shirt. Around his neck was the whale tooth pendant.

"When did you come back?" I asked.

"Eight, ten years ago. I don't remember. The years go by so fast. What are you doing here? Researching the strange habits of the natives?"

"Nope, this is strictly a holiday." I introduced him to Matt.

"Come. Let me buy you drinks at my family's place." He draped his arm over my shoulders and led us across the street to a funky, but inviting restaurant facing the waterfront.

We settled into chairs as a smiling young Polynesian woman approached for our orders. "This is my granddaughter Mari," said Mabata proudly. "Tell her what you want." We did so.

"I didn't think you'd ever tear yourself away from the Hollywood scene."

"That was no problem. I always planned to come back. My family is here. My ancestors are here. Where else could I live happily in my old age?"

"Do you still have family in the Tuamotus?"

"Some, but most of them are here in Tahiti now. My wife and all my children and grandchildren are here. Some brothers and sisters and lots of cousins, aunts and uncles. You know how it is with us Polynesians. We love our big families." He called three small boys over from their play. "These are my great-grandsons. This one's named Mabata—after me." The boys smiled shyly and then returned to their games.

"How many grandchildren and great-grandchildren do you have?"

He laughed. "I'm not sure. I haven't counted recently." His face brightened. "Here comes my wife. She's been shopping. I want you to meet her."

A large, older Polynesian woman wearing a bright blue muumuu entered the restaurant with four children in tow, all laden with produce from the market. Mabata spoke to her in what I assumed was a Tuamotu dialect. She came smilingly to our table.

"This is Hina, my long-suffering wife." We stood and acknowledged one another with smiles, sharing no common language.

"Tell her I'm very happy to meet her." She stayed a few minutes longer and then departed with her small entourage.

"Do you ever visit the States?" I asked.

"Not since I returned home. I have no interest in going back. Sometimes people from my Hollywood days pass through Papeete. It's always good to see them, but acting is in my past. It was good and allowed me to make money which made my family's life easier. But my life is full now. I sometimes help out here at the restaurant and I help my son who has a cruise boat for tourists. And the children always keep me busy. Frequently, the day is too short for everything I have to do."

We finished our drinks and Mabata insisted we come back that evening for dinner. It wasn't difficult to persuade us. We returned and ended up staying after midnight as the dinner stretched into an evening of drinking with visits from his large family.

Mabata suggested we join his son's cruise boat the following day. We were again easily persuaded. We visited Moorea, and then returned to Papeete for dinner at the family restaurant. Within the space of a week, Mabata made sure we saw most that Tahiti has to offer visitors. On the eve of our departure, he threw a party for us at his home, a spacious rambling open-air house at the edge of Papeete. His entire family was there as well as what seemed all the Polynesian population of Tahiti—plus a cosmopolitan collection of French, Chinese, Australians, New Zealanders and Americans. Food and drink flowed everywhere and the music and dancing never stopped.

We left Tahiti the following day and most of the party from the night before saw us off at the airport. Mabata's son chanted a friendship chant his father composed for me. Two of his grandsons, as magnificent as their grandfather in his youth, accompanied the chant with dance. I was moved and tears filled my eyes as I embraced Mabata long and warmly to let him know.

He looked at me, also with moist eyes, and said, "If we'd lived near one another, I think our friendship would've been much more."

"Yes. I think it would've been."

I departed Tahiti with great reluctance, as almost everyone who has visited that special island. Matt and I continued our journey across the South Pacific and a month later we were back in San Francisco.

One chilly foggy morning, a few weeks after I returned, I stumbled out of bed, brewed a steaming mug of coffee to clear sleep from my head and went online to check my email. At the top of the list was a note from Mabata's son. The message was brief: "I regret to inform you that my father died of a heart attack last week while entertaining friends in our restaurant. He spent his last hours with people who loved him. He did not suffer. He is buried with our ancestors."

I carried my coffee mug to the window and quietly gazed at the foggy city, listening to the moaning fog-horns as my memories of Mabata warmed the chilly San Francisco morning.

The Golden Imams

I ALWAYS KNEW CANCER would catch up with me someday. My genealogy is rather explicit about that. My great-grandfather brought the disease from Scotland and it appeared routinely in his family's succeeding generations in the United States. Nonetheless, I wasn't quite ready for it. I suppose one never is.

After discovering a tiny tumor in my lower colon, the medical establishment convinced me that chemotherapy combined with radiation was the appropriate treatment for destroying the growing malignancy within me. Someday people will be appalled that we once treated cancer patients with such savage methods of poisoning and burning their bodies. But that was the treatment I received.

I surrendered my body to the staff at my medical center. A very thin plastic tube was inserted into the major artery in the underside of my right forearm all the way to my heart. It was attached to a pump that fed a container of chemo to the targeted organ. For three days, it would pump chemo into my body. I was already measured and marked for the radiation rays that would target the tumor five times a week for six weeks beginning the same day I began the chemo. During the last three days of radiation, the chemo would be reattached for a final infusion.

The early days of chemo and radiation were a piece of cake and I began questioning the validity of all the horror stories I'd heard from others who'd experienced the treatment. However, after the first two weeks things began to change. The radiated area felt like a serious sunburn and each new day brought burn upon burn until my groin crackled with pain. Each morning I forced myself to the appointment and more searing pain. When I approached my last three days of radiation, the poisonous chemo and its pump were reattached. Meanwhile my hair was falling out and pounds were dropping from my body.

On the final day of the second round of chemo, I developed a high fever, weakened and slipped into unconsciousness. When I awakened, I was in a hospital bed hooked to tubes and watched by the anxious eyes of two friends dressed in protective white garb that kept their potential infections to themselves since I no longer had an immune system to fight them off. I was invaded by needles, tubes, drips and pills bequeathing me morphine, zolpidem, dolasetron, glucose, potassium and others I have forgotten or perhaps never knew.

Tests revealed that the chemo had consumed my blood platelets and transfusions were in order. A bag of sickly yellow liquid drained into my vein. I began to chill. I grew colder and shivered as the vile fluid invaded my body. I shook uncontrollably thinking they will surely stop the procedure. But they persisted and my shaking continued as I grew colder watching the anxious faces around me. Then I began slowly slipping away—away from the faces, away from the room, away to another place...

...I am in a boat on a river, the Solo River in Java. It is a small wooden boat and I am the only person aboard. I am standing at the prow naked. I am young and my body is beautiful. My red hair is long. The boat is unpainted and bleached by the sun. The water is muddy. I slowly pass houses on either side. Their windows are blank. They are tiled in pale shades of yellow, pink, blue, green and lavender. I see no people. The sun is bright. Tall green reeds choke the river leaving a narrow central passage for my boat. The prow pushes through the butterscotch-muddy waters as the passage becomes increasingly narrow. As I progress upstream, the reeds slowly change to pale green and then to yellow and eventually to gold. They shimmer in the water and in the sunlight as we pass the empty houses. All is silent. The reeds begin expanding, glittering and surrounding the boat. Slowly they become old Javanese men with warm brown faces smiling kindly, wearing golden robes and white turbans. They are imams. They do not speak but they know I am among them. They slowly part, allowing the passage of my boat. Their golden robes grow brighter and brighter, shimmering and glittering in the sunshine, hurting my eyes. The imams merge and surround me in golden warmth and then slowly move ahead effortlessly becoming a bright golden ball blinding me with its brilliance. Smaller golden balls transform into skulls

of Solo Man. They smile and encircle me. They do not frighten me. I ask the skulls, "Is any part of my life real or is it all simply a story I am making up? Or is it both? Maybe my life is merely a made-up tale created as I journey through my existence. There is no reality. I create reality as I live my life." My boat enters the golden ball and I am consumed by its brilliance. And then suddenly it explodes into trillions of tiny particles. And all the gold is gone. Only darkness remains . . .

. . . I opened my eyes to the brilliant white hospital room. Eight days later I was discharged from the hospital to rebuild my body and reclaim my life.

For Auld Lang Syne

I'VE NEVER ATTENDED a New Year's Eve party. The noise, the drunkenness, the crowds—none of that for me. I prefer my own quiet end-of-the-year ritual all by myself. It begins with oyster stew prepared the way my mother prepared it: half milk, half cream, fresh oysters, minced celery, a little butter and healthy dashes of salt and pepper. When ready, the stew goes into a white bowl sprinkled with oyster crackers. Some soft Mozart or Beethoven, piano or violin, provides background listening. After consuming the stew, I go to the library and pull a volume of Tennyson's poetry from the bookshelf. I settle into my reading chair and leaf through the book until I find "In Memoriam." I locate Canto CVI of the wordy poem that begins:

> *Ring out, wild bells, to the wild sky,*
> *The flying cloud, the frosty light:*
> *The year is dying in the night;*
> *Ring out, wild bells, and let him die.*

The canto continues for seven more stanzas, anticipating the promising new year and celebrating the end of the disappointing old one. I reflect on the lines, contemplate past years and past people, and then retire long before the stroke of midnight.

But this year, my seventy-fifth, I decided to break tradition and throw a New Year's Eve party for a group of people once close to me, people I hadn't seen in a long time.

My housekeeper cleaned the flat earlier in the week so I needn't worry about tidying up for the guests. Oyster stew is easy, so no problem there. We would congregate late and usher in the new year together. I began planning where I would seat my guests.

I added a leaf to the dining table and covered it with a white lace tablecloth crocheted by my grandmother long before I was born. I arranged the yellow roses I bought that afternoon into a simple display in the dime-store vase I gave my mother on her birthday when I was ten years old. I set places for seven—more than seven usually breaks down into smaller conversation units. I wanted us all together. I placed white Wedgwood soup bowls around the table, polished the Waterford champagne glasses and set them beside the bowls. Nothing but the best for this party. Soup spoons were the only flatware needed and I positioned them on the white linen napkins beside the bowls. Two white candles in crystal holders in the middle of the table and a log burning in the fireplace provided the only illumination in the room. A CD of Beethoven's "Moonlight Sonata" added to the ambiance. I went to the library and read the Tennyson verses. After contemplating the familiar lines, I returned to the dining room with the photos I sorted from my collection that afternoon. I sat at the head of the table.

I placed Garth across the table from me. He wore a magenta turban that unsuccessfully controlled his blond hair and beard. The photo was taken during his fieldwork in Thailand. Garth and I were fellow graduate students in anthropology. He was my first openly gay friend, back in the days when it was not okay to be gay. Garth was a big man, strong and masculine and unashamedly gay. While I was doing PhD fieldwork in the southern Philippines, he did archeology in the far north of Thailand, discovering dates that would rewrite the history of agriculture in Southeast Asia.

After graduate studies, we found academic jobs in California within easy driving distance of one another. He was on the threshold of a brilliant career when he discovered a tiny mole on his back that was diagnosed as melanoma. He was terrified when he learned the diagnosis. Then as the disease spread, his terror transformed to anger. He didn't want to die and was determined to beat the disease. Oncologists told him what he refused to believe: nothing could be done to stop the cancer. He traveled to Germany in search of a cure by an old gypsy woman he discovered through his grapevine of fellow melanoma sufferers. Then he learned about a holy man in Bombay and went there seeking treatment. In New York City, he found a man from Mali who claimed success in curing cancer with mysterious herbs. They traveled together several months, concocting vile brews which Garth religiously drank several times a day. A shaman in Guatemala offered cures when he and Garth were in trance together. When I last saw Garth, he was emaciated and bitter, still determined the disease would not claim his big life. A week later he died en route to New Mexico where he planned to visit a celebrated *curandero*. I looked at his wide smile and intense blue eyes and wondered how Garth would have changed archeology had he lived.

A good mother takes you a long way in life. I had a great mom. And I wasn't the only one who thought so. Everyone liked my mom. I smiled at her face in the photo, the face I remembered when I was about twelve. I placed her on my left.

Mom was plumpish with dark hair and warm dark eyes and a ready smile. She was a great cook, managed to put together a complete dinner at noon and an equally complete supper in the evening. Dad quietly brought home the paycheck each week and enjoyed the lively household Mom created. I don't know how she did it all—cooking, baking, laundry, ironing, canning and housecleaning. In my childhood memories, she was constantly working at something but she always ended the day reading the newspaper before she went to bed. And she always had time to talk about whatever presented itself. I never thought much about it at the time but I now realize she was a very bright woman. I might harbor regrets that her education ended at high school (which wasn't bad back in that time and place) and she never had the opportunity to attend college which she would've loved. But her life was fulfilled. Many family problems came to our house for her counsel and many a sick child was brought for her advice and nurturance.

As I grew older, I looked forward to knowing Mom in her old age. She was a wise woman and I anticipated hearing her elder wisdom. That didn't happen. She acquired Alzheimer's disease in her mid-sixties. We kept her at home until she didn't know where she was and recognized no one. Then we placed her in a care facility where she received the watchful care she needed. For nine years she vegetated as we painfully watched this wonderful woman retreat into a world that excluded us.

She was hospitalized with pneumonia and the family was called to her bedside. As she breathed her last breaths, she suddenly opened her eyes and looked at us with a big smile. Then she quietly died. I like to believe that in that final glimpse she recognized her children and was again the mother we once knew.

I picked up Duncan's photo and looked at his melancholy face. Duncan and I were brothers, very different from one another but with that special bond brothers sometimes have. After fifty years it still hurts so much. I used to think it would go away, but I know now it never will.

Why did you do it Duncan? I've asked that question so many times. You missed so much. Fifty years of living and still counting. Each time I read or hear of a suicide, I seek privacy for the tears I know will come. I never realized that hurts can last a lifetime. They talk about closure, but there's no closure. You learn to live with the pain, but sometimes it comes flooding back and hurts all over again. Surely you would never have done it if you knew you would hurt us so much.

If I learned anything from your suicide, I learned that I could never do what you did. I could never inflict such pain on the ones who love me. We went on with our lives but there will always be that raw emptiness within each of us. A part of us died with you. I blinked away tears and placed Duncan's photo at Garth's left.

Jake was a nice guy. Everyone thought so. A quiet man with a shy smile, he was a trucker who drove twice weekly round trips from San Francisco to L.A. I met him when he married the sister of one of my friends. He had only a high school education and was always somewhat uncomfortable around the educated people he sometimes found himself among. His wife was a tiny, fragile woman who was diagnosed with muscular sclerosis in their third year of marriage. She deteriorated rapidly and within six months of diagnosis was in a wheelchair. One Sunday morning while she was watching television in her bedroom and Jake was in the kitchen washing dishes, she choked to death on a piece of toast.

Jake was devastated. He slipped into a deep depression and retired early from his job. As he slowly crawled out of his depression, he explored possibilities for the next chapter of his life. He spent three months in Acapulco but found little except alcohol in the beachside bars. After sobering up back in L.A., he tried the Big Island in Hawaii, but discovered only loneliness. Then one day he met another retiree who was headed for the Philippines where he'd spent time during his navy days. He invited

Jake to join him. Jake did so but it didn't work out and they went their separate ways in Baguio.

While plotting his next move, he met a Filipina waitress in one of the local hotels where he took his meals. I don't think they fell in love, but they liked one another well enough to start sleeping together, then living together and then marriage when she became pregnant. Both tired of the sometimes chilly Baguio climate and decided to move to the wife's village in rural Cebu where she had a big extended family. Jake loved his new family and he and his wife added to it. After their first child, two more followed in as many years. I visited Jake during one of my trips to the Philippines and he was happy as a clam. Social Security and pension checks allowed him to live in the upper echelons of Cebuano society.

One morning a few months after the birth of his third child, he got out of bed, dressed, bent over to tie his shoe and died of a stroke. A tragic end, perhaps. But maybe not so tragic. His final years were the happiest of his life. Not bad, Jake. For many people, those last years are the unhappiest. You always remind me that there's more to come, and maybe it'll be the best. I placed him beside Mom.

Where did you go Grandma Miller? After all these years I still wonder. I looked at her photo. She wasn't really my grandmother, but everyone in the little town where I grew-up called her "Grandma Miller." In fact, I don't think she was anyone's grandmother. She was widowed shortly after her marriage and her only son was killed in the war. The quintessential grandmother, she was plump, kind and sweet with white hair and bright blue eyes. She lived a block down the street from my family in a little three-room house. As a small child I liked to visit her for the candy she always gave me and as I grew older, I helped mow her lawn, weed her garden, rake her leaves and shovel snow from her sidewalks. She was a marvelous raconteur and I loved hearing her stories.

Born in 1875, she spent her youth on a farm during the waning days of the Iowa frontier. Her stories were living history lessons for me. She remembered when the first automobile appeared, when she saw her first airplane and heard her first radio broadcast. She had fond memories of winter sleigh rides and summer hayrides pulled by teams of horses, noisy thrashing machines harvesting the wheat, bands of Indians occasionally appearing on her family farm, barn raisings and quilting bees, and her one-room country schoolhouse—and the excitement when her home acquired electricity and its first telephone.

She frequently told me she hated wars, that they were horrible. Then she would pause with a catch in her throat and I was afraid she was going to cry because I knew her brother was killed in the Great War and her son was killed in the second one. But I never saw her cry, although her eyes sometimes welled with tears. She had no relatives in our little town, but she didn't seem lonely. Everyone liked her and she had frequent visitors. As many of her generation, her independence was important to her. She once told me she was concerned that she might become a burden to someone when she grew old. At the time, I remember thinking that she was already old.

When I entered high school, I saw less of Grandma Miller but I stopped by her house regularly to see if she needed help with anything. During my junior year, her health began deteriorating and her vitality and sparkle faded. Her sparsely furnished house was becoming sparser as she gave away household items to friends and neighbors. She told me she was sorting things out and organizing her affairs so no one would have to do it after her death. Her impending death increasingly became a reality to me.

One November Saturday morning I stopped by to see Grandma Miller and noticed a suitcase on her couch. When I asked if she was going somewhere, she told me she decided to visit a cousin in Chicago. I was puzzled. She'd never mentioned any cousin before and I'd never known her to be away from home overnight. She said she'd recently turned eighty and it was time to take the trip while she was still able. She asked if I'd carry her suitcase to the Sinclair gas station a few blocks away where the Greyhound bus stopped every morning at eleven. I agreed to do so. We left her house and met several neighbors along the way who were surprised to see the suitcase. When they asked where she was going, she said she was taking a little trip she'd planned for some time. At the Sinclair station we had only a short wait before the bus arrived. When it pulled up, she took her suitcase and thanked me for always being so kind to her. She said I was a good boy and she knew I was going to have a good life—and to my embarrassment she kissed me on the cheek before boarding the bus.

Several weeks after she left, a letter arrived at our school from Grandma Miller addressed to the principal. It stated that her house and everything in it were to be sold and the money from the sale should go to the school. The letter had no return address but it was postmarked "Chicago." County and state officials were eventually notified of her disappearance and a statewide and then a nationwide search were conducted but she was never located. Many stories circulated throughout town about her possible whereabouts but none were ever confirmed.

I still wonder where you went Grandma Miller. I hope it was a good place. If you'd stayed home, we would've cared for you. I placed her photo on the right of me.

Diane was bright and beautiful, not beautiful in a traditional pretty way but handsome in a strikingly memorable way. We were grad students together, she in art history and I in anthropology. We hung out at the same lefty student bar with mutual friends mulling over the weighty problems of the world and offering our often naïve solutions to them.

During the course of our friendship, Diane fell in love with me. I guess I fell in love with her too. I wasn't sure what love was back in those days—not sure I do now—and didn't know how to react when she told me she loved me. She was the first straight person I told I was gay. I didn't want to lead her on and didn't want to lie to her, but I didn't want to lose her friendship. So I told her I was gay. Back then gay wasn't an acceptable way to be, even among university intellectuals. I later learned she wasn't entirely surprised but she'd hoped otherwise. Our relationship cooled. A few weeks later, she flew to Paris for six months of PhD research. I wrote her a couple of times, but she didn't respond and I assumed it was over. I was sad because I liked her a lot.

The week she returned to campus she called and asked me to meet her at our old drinking place. She looked great. Paris was good to her. After about an hour of catching-up, she told me she still loved me. My expression was telling. She laughed and quickly added, "Not that way," and explained that she considered me her best friend and wanted to keep it that way. I agreed. We remained great friends and occasionally traveled together through the vicissitudes of our long lives. She died suddenly a year ago of an aneurism. I've often thought if I'd been straight and we'd married, we'd probably never had the beautiful friendship we did. Not too many marriages result in that. Thanks Diane. I'm glad we never married. I placed her photo beside Grandma Miller.

The grandfather clock in the entry hall began striking. Outside, the night burst into the New Year accompanied by a cacophony of honking horns, pealing bells, rowdy revelers and exploding fireworks. I stood and quietly raised my champagne glass to the noisy night. I sipped the champagne, raised my glass again and whispered to the assembled photos, "For Auld Lang Syne . . . for Auld Lang Syne . . . for Auld Lang Syne."

Books by H. Arlo Nimmo

FICTION

The Songs of Salanda

A Very Far Place

Before Summer

Night Train

NON-FICTION

The Sea People of Sulu

The Bajau of the Philippines

Directions in Pacific Traditional Literature
(Co-edited with Adrienne L. Kaeppler)

The Pele Literature

*Magosaha: An Ethnography of the
Tawi-Tawi Sama Dilaut*

The Andrews Sisters

*Good and Bad Times in a
San Francisco Neighborhood*

Pele, Volcano Goddess of Hawaii

53769422R00122

Made in the USA
San Bernardino, CA
28 September 2017